Francie Again

STARLIGHT NOVELS

BIG BRIGHT LAND
by Enid Johnson and Anne Merriman Peck

CARNIVAL GYPSY
by Dorothy Gilman Butters

CATCHPENNY STREET
by Elizabeth Headley

ENCHANTED CARAVAN
by Dorothy Gilman Butters

FRANCIE
by Emily Hahn

FRANCIE AGAIN
by Emily Hahn

LINDA'S HOMECOMING
by Phyllis A. Whitney

PUPPY STAKES
by Betty Cavanna

REMEMBER THE VALLEY
by Nora Benjamin

SHE'S MY GIRL
by Elizabeth Headley

SHOESTRING THEATER
by Nancy Hartwell

SPRING COMES RIDING
by Betty Cavanna

TAKE A CALL, TOPSY!
by Elizabeth Headley

By EMILY HAHN

Francie Again

GROSSET & DUNLAP *Publishers*

NEW YORK

Francie Again

CLOUDS held them up at Le Bourget. The plane circled around in the mystifying manner of its kind, so that a few passengers were able joyfully to point out landmarks to each other but then lost sight of them temporarily and were angry with the pilot when they spotted them again, farther away. However, the hostess said everything was under control, and she obviously meant it.

It had been a rough crossing, and habit, not vanity, made Francie look at her reflection in her compact mirror. She had seldom cared less how she looked. She had been tossed around, her legs were cramped from sitting still, and the air was stuffy in spite of the air-conditioning system she had been reading about during the past hour, for want of something better, in the glossy booklet of the air company.

It seemed years since she had been happily excited about boarding the plane in New York and embarking on this adventure. Everything was different after a nearly sleepless night. She scarcely dared look ahead to the winter which had seemed so lovely before, when Aunt Lolly's letter arrived and she read it in Pop's hotel apartment. Only the present was actual, and that seemed grimy, though the plane was the air line's pride and the people on the passenger list had possessed nearly as much glamour—yesterday—as their impossibly soignée prototypes in the booklet illustrations. That woman across the aisle, for example, who said she was going to France on a buying trip for her Fifth Avenue employers: yesterday at the New York airport she had been as smart and impeccable as if she had just arrived from Paris, rather than being on the way there, but now she looked dowdy and cross.

"About as dowdy and cross as I do myself," Francie reflected. Thinking of her own childish scowl, she laughed and immediately felt better. There was no reason in the world for bad temper, unless hunger and sleepiness could excuse it. Nobody was ever in a better spot, she thought. With the career she wanted ahead of her and plenty of friends to help her on the way, with Aunt Lolly waiting for her, no doubt only a few hundred yards away this minute, and Paris for the winter, and the famous Plessis' studio to work in, could any girl want more? Well, yes— food would be very nice.

Also, she felt just a bit uncertain about things in general. At eighteen, most people would not mind uncertainty, and when Francie was normally fed and rested she didn't, either. But now, in one swift gloomy moment, she could not help remembering an earlier time of upheaval, not quite a year before, when she had been suddenly whisked away from home and plunked down in an English boarding school. It had all turned out for the best, but oh, those first few days at Fairfields School! Still, it *had* turned out for the best, and this time was different. This time she would not be on her own, but visiting darling Aunt Lolly, who made it home wherever she was.

"And this time," thought Francie, "I'm different myself. I've found myself. I know what I want to *do* in life."

She was going to be a great painter. That was settled—at least it was settled for Francie and she had met with no obstacles from the two people who directed her life. Pop, her father, wasn't opposed to the idea at all.

"If that's what you want to do," said Pop, "I guess the sooner you go ahead with it the better. I don't like the way some kids hang around doing nothing."

That was Pop's way—quick, decided, and, if the truth were told, just a bit absent-minded. Francie always said he didn't ever really wake up unless he was talking to somebody connected with the oil business. It was a family joke between them.

The only other person who had influence over Francie was Laura Barclay, her Aunt Lolly—an aunt-by-courtesy, really. She had been the best friend of Francie's mother, and, as the girl could not herself remember her mother, she knew how lucky she was to have such an understanding older woman to depend on.

Aunt Lolly *was* dependable, said Francie to herself. She was better than that; she often turned up with glamorous plans that somehow fitted in beautifully with Francie's serious desires or ambitions. How like her it was, when she found out that her husband Martin Barclay was to be in Paris for a year on United Nations business, to remember a talk she had had with Francie about Plessis.

Francie had said, "He's the best teacher in the world. I'd give anything to study under him for a while! But I don't guess I'll have any such luck for years. Pop says he won't let me go and live alone in Paris until I'm older."

It was like Aunt Lolly not to have forgotten, and to have written straight off to Mr. Nelson when she knew she could offer Francie a home. Thinking about her, Francie's shreds of ill humor vanished. At the same moment the plane made up its mind really to land, at last. They came down gently, rode along a sunny field, and halted.

Francie glanced again into the compact mirror, refreshed her lipstick, tugged at her hat, and smiled at the Fifth Avenue buyer. The looking-glass reflection had done its part to cheer her up. She was bright-eyed and fresh in spite of the bad night, and she still liked the looks of the blouse she had bought on Fourteenth Street and made over, just before she took the plane. Pop had been a little startled by the effect, but she was sure it was good. Yes, thought Francie, she might yet be able to face the critical eyes of Paris (for of course everyone in Paris *would* be critical) without shaming Aunt Lolly, or feeling apologetic about her education. After all, it was perfectly good Middle Western Jefferson, and it had a thin veneer of England. Aunt Lolly would help wherever necessary. Aunt Lolly would tell her if her appearance or behavior needed moderating. Francie took comfort in this thought, as she always did. Laura Barclay would never allow her to make a spectacle of herself in Paris.

"How slow they are," said the buyer. "This is always the worst of arriving by plane, isn't it?"

"Always," said Francie, hoping she sounded bored and experienced. Actually it was her first long plane voyage and her first time in France, but she had no desire to confess such matters to any of the other passengers. They all seemed blasé about Europe; they were people of the world. She didn't want them to look down on her as a gushing teen-ager.

Then at last the door opened, the air hostess stood at attention by it, and the passengers filed out to the welcome sun, glittering on France.

Slowly descending the steel steps at the heels of the Fifth Avenue buyer, Francie looked eagerly toward the crowd of welcomers who stood beyond the barrier. This was Europe again—Europe, which she had not expected to visit again for years. It wasn't England, but still it was the other half of the world, and for a second she had the experience, so difficult to describe, of seeming to be a much earlier self, wearing another, well-remembered shell of personality. She was Francie the schoolgirl, a stranger, homesick in England. Then she glanced down at her pretty suit, her reassuring shoes and slim nylon ankles. No, she was today's Francie, thank goodness—no faltering schoolgirl but a well-bred young woman, coming to Paris to visit the popular Mrs. Barclay.

Incidentally, where *was* the popular Mrs. Barclay? She should have been there in the front row, smiling and waving. The passengers came close to the barrier and Francie scanned the crowd carefully, face by face, but no Aunt Lolly was there.

"Oh well, she's probably had trouble parking," she decided, and went through the gate. She had not looked at the men in the crowd, so she was startled when a man seized her arm and said, "There you are, young woman, and about time, too. I thought you were never coming down to earth."

"Oh, Uncle Martin! I was just beginning to think I was deserted. Aunt Lolly's outside, is she?"

"No, she's at home waiting for you. Come on, we'll have to get you through the customs," said Martin Barclay. Francie followed him meekly while he found her luggage and talked to the *douaniers*. People always deferred to Uncle Martin, because in his easy way he seemed to be used to deference. Today, however, he looked preoccupied and grave. She wondered what might be the trouble.

Then she dismissed her misgivings and turned to look at France, or at as much of it as she could see in the shed. It all looked very much like the pictures. Dark-eyed, vivacious people talked to each other excitedly, and now and then she could make out a word, but it was clear that her school French was not going to be adequate for her needs. Uncle Martin's French, however, was fine. It had a quickening effect on everybody. Long before the Fifth Avenue buyer was released, Francie and Uncle Martin were driving in his car toward Paris.

Away from the traffic confusion at the field, Francie

felt free to ask, "Is anything the matter, Uncle Martin?"

"Well, yes, there is," he replied. "It's nothing really to worry about, but your Aunt Lolly isn't well."

Francie exclaimed in dismay, "I knew there was something!"

"It's not serious," Uncle Martin went on, "except that it makes her so uncomfortable. She's quite crippled, temporarily. Arthritis of some sort in her hip, they told us at the American Hospital. She's relieved, though, to find she'll be all right if she takes care. That's going to be the difficulty. You know what she is."

"You should have let me know," said Francie. "I'll bet it's been bothering her to think about me coming just now and making a lot of trouble."

"Not at all! You'll probably do her a lot of good."

"I hope so," said Francie, gloomily. She couldn't remember that Aunt Lolly had ever been ill before. France was forgotten and she ignored the flat countryside, though she had intended to look at everything during this momentous first drive. Uncle Martin, however, cheered up after unburdening himself.

"Well, young lady, haven't you anything new to tell us? I thought you'd be wearing an engagement ring by this time."

"Me? Don't be silly, Uncle Martin. Who would I be engaged to?"

Uncle Martin said, "Your old reliable, of course. What's-his-name, that snub-nosed kid in Jefferson. Glenn, that's it."

"Glenn!" From Francie's tone, one would have thought Glenn was the last person in the world she had ever considered. Yet she was not displeased. She smiled in spite of herself.

"Haven't forgotten him in the big city, have you?" asked Uncle Martin with pretended anxiety.

"Oh no, we correspond. But to think of *Glenn*! I mean—oh, look!" She broke off with a cry of pleasure at sight of the chestnut trees that line the Avenue de Marigny. "Oh, what a beautiful neighborhood! Do you live here? How lucky!"

"It's not too bad," said Uncle Martin. He stopped the car in front of a stone house. "Now then, Francie, if you'll ring the bell so the *concierge* will let us in— that's it. Just pull the handle."

A bell rang far inside the door, and after a pause an old woman shuffled out. She spoke shrilly to Uncle Martin, then shuffled back indoors to shout up the stairs Francie saw beyond her in the gloom. It all seemed old-fashioned in an unfamiliar way that was yet evocative. "I can *almost* remember places like it," thought Francie, "probably from books or pictures."

A younger servant came running downstairs. She smiled at Francie as she picked up the heaviest suitcase, and went indoors. "You go along with her," commanded Uncle Martin. "That's our maid Félice. Tell your aunt I'll be up right away."

"What a funny arrangement," Francie said to herself, "like the Middle Ages, keeping a guard at the door of your own house." She followed the maid up a dark narrow stairway.

"Francie, darling!"

There was Aunt Lolly—oh dear, there was poor Aunt Lolly coming across the floor of a big room, limping on a stick and leaning way over. It was a drawing room with a high ceiling, and gilded mirrors that reached all the way up the wall. They magnified the room enormously. Several Aunt Lollies seemed to limp across the soft carpet.

Aunt Lolly hugged her with one arm, leaning on the stick with the other. "It *is* good to see you, my dear. I can't give you a proper welcome, crippled like this. Isn't it infuriating? Uncle Martin told you, I suppose? What a shame this is! I did so want to come to the airport to meet you, but I simply couldn't. I've already canceled everything else this afternoon, and suppose someone had seen me after I'd sent regrets? It's the kind of thing that invariably happens."

"You couldn't possibly have come, Aunt Lolly. I think it's a rotten shame this has happened to you. You should have put me off, you know you should."

"What nonsense the child talks!" Aunt Lolly sat

down on an elegant little sofa, making room for Francie. "I'm not really laid up or at death's door or anything like that."

Yet she was thinner than when Francie had last seen her in England, and there were dark circles under her eyes.

"I wouldn't have dreamed of putting you off, especially as I'd already upset all your plans for the winter. It does me a world of good to see you. Here, let's look at you." She drew back and scrutinized Francie, and said, "You've grown up."

"It's my American clothes, that's all," said Francie. "Quite a change from that dismal Sunday frock model we all wore at Fairfields, isn't it?" She glanced down at herself with a touch of complacence, wondering if Aunt Lolly would notice the blouse. Aunt Lolly did.

"What's that enchanting pattern you're wearing?" she demanded.

"I picked it out of practically a rubbish heap. Do you like it? I love it myself—worked at it all night," said Francie. "It's such a new kind of color. Sort of weird."

"You have a flair," said Mrs. Barclay thoughtfully.

"But Aunt Lolly, what does the doctor say about you?"

"Oh, my dear, that's what's so awful. I would have written to you at great length if only there had been time, but perhaps on the whole it's as well I didn't. Otherwise I'm not sure—Oh good, darling," she broke off in a relieved way as Uncle Martin came in. "You're just in time. I haven't yet broken the news to Francie."

Uncle Martin said, "Oh." He sat down.

Francie, looking from one to the other, was alarmed again. Her first thought was that they had got bad news from Pop. She said impulsively, "Is it something about New York? But I've only just left there!"

Aunt Lolly took her hand. "No, no, dear, of course not. It's something else. I'm afraid we'll have to disappoint you cruelly. I do feel ashamed of being such a bother."

Uncle Martin cut in. "Your aunt's not supposed to stay in Paris this winter," he said. "The doctor's very definite about it. He says she must go somewhere sunny and warm, somewhere warmer than here, and stay right through until summer. It can get pretty darn cold in Paris."

"So we decided on Portugal," said Aunt Lolly. "It's gay there, and I think you'll like it."

"Me?" Until this minute, Francie had not thought how the news would affect herself. But now that Aunt Lolly had said it, she realized that it was inevitable. Pop had refused to let her come to Paris and live here by herself, and now that Aunt Lolly wouldn't be here—Oh, it *was* a disappointment! No

Paris, no art classes with Plessis, the whole academic year lost! From the heights of bliss Francie fell with a bump.

"Poor child. I'm so sorry," said Aunt Lolly. "I know what it means to you. It really is a shame."

"We wondered if maybe you'd rather go on with your course in New York after all," said Uncle Martin, "but it's kind of late in the day to change that, I guess. Anyway for this term."

Francie had to steady her voice before replying.

"I don't think they'd let me come in now. They've been in session a couple of weeks already."

"No, I was afraid of that," said Uncle Martin. "Anyway, to tell you the truth I'm just as glad, for selfish reasons. If you weren't here your aunt would have had to stay in Portugal by herself. I could have managed to go along and settle her in, but I couldn't have stayed. Now if you're with her—"

"Martin, you know that's not necessary," said Mrs. Barclay. "I can manage beautifully by myself. Portuguese servants are very kind and helpful. If Francie would rather go back to America and carry on with her studies I'd understand perfectly, and so would her father, I'm sure."

She meant it, Francie knew that. Aunt Lolly was always thoughtful and genuine. And it would be more pleasant for herself, she was sure, to go back to Pop and find some way of carrying on with the work she liked so much. There were private teachers. A whole year wasted in Portugal! But—

She stole a glance at Uncle Martin. He looked worried. He was hoping, hard, that she would go with Aunt Lolly. Francie suppressed a sigh, and said,

"I want to stay with you, of course, Aunt Lolly, if you'll have me."

"Good girl," said Uncle Martin.

CHAPTER 2

THE windows reached to the top of the room, a long way above head height. When they were unobscured they looked on a wonderful near-emptiness of blue sea and blue sky. You could pull them open enough to squeeze halfway out, Francie had learned, to a little ornamental metal balcony. You couldn't go farther because there was simply nowhere to stand, but it was a good place there between the room and the sea. It was a wonderful place to stand and brood, romantically and sorrowfully, about life's buffets.

Unfortunately the hotel chambermaid didn't seem to understand that windows were for opening. She carried on relentless war against fresh air and light. First thing in the morning when she came in with Francie's chocolate she would go and close not only the glass casements but the little shutters inside them. When Francie objected, she pretended not to understand. Perhaps she really didn't, because Francie's Portuguese was scanty. The maid would say something about heat, and sunlight in the middle of the day, and then she would pull down a sunblind behind the shutter before she went out.

"It's a Portuguese custom," Aunt Lolly said when Francie complained. "They think the room is cooler if you never open the shutters. And really, dear, they might possibly be right. They've lived here, you know, all their lives."

Francie sighed with impatience, but complained no more. She went back to her room and opened the window for the tenth time.

It wasn't fair to bother Aunt Lolly, especially as the change of scene and air seemed to be doing her a lot of good. They had been in Estoril, the seaside suburb of Lisbon, for little more than a fortnight, but already Mrs. Barclay was getting about, now and then, without her cane. It was the sun, she said gratefully. She could feel it sinking into her bones and comforting them.

One afternoon Francie squeezed out on the balcony and peered down at the sandy ribbon that curled around the hotel's feet and stretched down the coast. On one side stood an ancient fort. On the other, the beach disappeared beyond an immense white turreted palace with its own private pier. Francie knew what it was like beyond. She knew all this stretch of coast. She had walked up and down as far as she had time to go between meals, or on decorous outings with Aunt Lolly. She knew the electric train line and the well-barbered gardens with their palm trees, and the dignified little villas, and the tame little hills. It was all very Los Angeles, she told herself. Not that she disliked California, when she was there! But one hadn't come to Europe just for this.

"Anyway, what *do* I want?" she demanded, bored with her own discontent. "I'm having a very good time. All these friends of Aunt Lolly's are very nice. It would have been just the same in Paris, really."

But would it? Of course, even in Paris she wouldn't have been allowed to lead the deliciously adventurous life she had vaguely imagined back in New York. In Paris, as here, her companions would have been friends of the Barclays, sober, quiet-living gentlefolk and their quiet, well-behaved young daughters and sons. But still it would have been Paris, a magic name, whereas Francie had never even heard of Estoril until a month ago.

"And in Paris I'd have been hard at work by this time," she added. "Here I'm just playing around. Tennis and golf and cards, and not really a terrific rush even so. That's another thing; it seems to me people are awfully slow-moving in Portugal. They seem too peaceful."

Again she peered at the sand, disapprovingly, for it was hushed and deserted at three in the afternoon. In Estoril, most people liked to rest after a long, late lunch. At four, she knew, there would be a change when Portugal woke up. Then the beach would suddenly be thronged.

"I think I'll go swimming right now," she resolved, "before I'm crowded out and stared at." She put on her bathing suit and robe and hurried down to the beach door. It had been the subject of some argument with Mrs. Barclay as to whether a young girl ought to go out alone in this manner. Aunt Lolly said Francie should behave like the Portuguese girls they had heard of in Paris, who were carefully chaperoned everywhere they went.

"But you can't go around with me," Francie pointed out, "because it's bad for you. And I'm not Portuguese, and they're used to foreigners behaving in their own way. Phyllis Wilkinson goes around on her own."

It was a telling argument. Phyllis was the daughter of one of Aunt Lolly's English acquaintances who were resident in Portugal.

"If you're sure," said Aunt Lolly uncertainly.

"Positive."

So now, with a clear conscience, Francie stepped

out to the beach, where the sand was hot enough to feel glowing even through the rope soles of her sandals. She dropped her towel and robe, and waded in for the first long swim of the afternoon. The water was cool for such a warm day, and as she went in deeper, moving slowly along the shallows, she felt her querulousness ebbing away. She swam straight out from the tall, civilized façade of the hotel, until at last she was satisfied and rolled over to paddle idly along with a backstroke, eyes closed against the sun.

Over there beyond the shoreline, she mused, was a foreign country that held all kinds of possibilities. She was eager to know more than the countryside she had seen during the little motor tours she and Mrs. Barclay had taken, though that was fascinating. She wanted to know what the people were like. It was not enough to see them, moving against the hills or harbors in their opera-chorus clothes, though all that was thrilling. What were they really like?

It seemed hopeless that she should ever find out. Portugal, for an American girl living in a luxury hotel in Estoril, might as well be Florida. Those peasant girls in their black or red skirts and gold necklaces, those fishermen had their own lives and cared nothing for hers. As for the middle-class Portuguese, nobody ever got to know them—the English had told her so. It was no use trying; Francie was typed. She was merely one more of the foreigners who invaded the city and made it look like every city in the world.

Francie began to swim back slowly to shore. Beyond the hotel, up a steep, stone-built bank, she saw the main highway to Lisbon. A few cars like shiny monsters whizzed past, high above her head. Farther back were the electric train tracks, and then came little villas, pink or green or cream, scattered among the hills. It was pretty and it was dull. Francie turned again to the sea, and for reassurance looked at the old fort that had stood there in the water for centuries.

"I'd like to paint that," she thought, "only I bet every single visitor does it."

The only thing to do, she decided as she left the water, was to make the best of it, enjoy her stay as much as possible in the ordinary, conventional way, and look forward to the future when Aunt Lolly would be well enough to go back to Paris. Release was bound to come sooner or later, she reflected. In the meantime, there were plenty of girls in Jefferson and New York who wouldn't mind changing places with her. And that was putting it mildly.

Thinking deeply, she walked as if in a dream across the hard-packed wet sand and then on the dry, looser stuff toward the place where she had left her towel and bathrobe. At least she assumed it was the same place; she wasn't really thinking. At the back of her mind was a happy confidence that her clothes were the only ones on the beach. She picked up the white robe.

"Excuse me," said a gentle voice.

Francie was realizing with embarrassment at the same moment that it wasn't her robe at all. The towel and slippers lying underneath it were unfamiliar.

"Oh, *sorry*."

She looked up and saw a girl standing there smiling—a dark-haired girl, wearing a dark bathing suit and carrying her rubber cap in her hand, all wet and fresh from the sea. Beyond, Francie's own clothes lay where she had left them.

"It doesn't matter at all," said the other girl. There was a touch of accent in her speech.

"I thought they were mine, you see," said Francie.

"Naturally. Our wraps are the same," said the girl. "And as we are the only people on the beach—"

"But I was stupid. I mean, I wasn't really looking," said Francie. It seemed to her that she had pretty well exhausted the subject, though she didn't want to stop talking. Francie liked talking to people she encountered by herself, but in a foreign country like this she felt shy of pushing such a chance acquaintance. She was just moving on when the girl said quickly, as if to detain her,

"The water is good today, isn't it? Not too warm."

So Francie sat down on the sand with her, and they talked.

"I've made a friend," Francie announced to Aunt Lolly. Her voice was full of triumphant excitement.

"My goodness. By yourself?" asked Mrs. Barclay. They were drinking lemonade instead of tea, in the dim coolness of the patient's bedroom. Aunt Lolly usually spent most of the day quietly in bed.

"By myself, in the most unexpected way. She was swimming alone, the way I was. You see, Aunt Lolly, you and I were all wrong. She's actually a young Portuguese girl, but she was all alone, just the same."

"I think it must be unusual," said Aunt Lolly.

Francie confessed, "It was, as a matter of fact. I guess her mother let her do it because it was the quiet, unfashionable time of day, and she was right inside the hotel lounge all the time—her mother, I mean, sitting there with some aunts or something. This girl Maria is more independent than most of them. She's been to America for a visit. Isn't that queer?"

"Not particularly, dear. Lots of people go to America."

"Yes, I know, but I mean it's queer we should have started to talk. Her name's Maria da Souza. She has other names too, but she said that will do to go on with. Portuguese names are terribly hard to remember at first." Francie drank the last sugary drops of her lemonade. "If you don't mind, I'm going back to join them now," she said. "They're staying at this hotel for a week or two—Maria and her mother and a brother named Ruy, and she wants me to meet them. It really is luck, isn't it?—running into the one Portuguese girl in the whole place who knows about America. Maria's crazy about New York."

Francie had taken care when she dressed, but when she saw Maria's family sitting straight-backed and neat in a row, waiting in the lounge, she felt unkempt, nevertheless. It was a feeling she was not used to, but there it was. There was something impeccable about Portuguese women; she had noticed it before, from a distance. On the hottest days they always looked crisp and cool. And their hair! However did they manage to keep it so neat?

Three da Souzas were there: Maria, her mother Dona Gracia (a lovely name, Francie thought) and her brother Ruy. Dona Gracia and Maria were in white linen, and the young man was in white, too. They looked alike, all three of them, with their smooth shining hair and wide green eyes. It was difficult at first to think of anything to converse about. In the presence of her mother Maria wasn't as chatty as she had been on the beach.

"We are sorry to hear that your aunt is unwell," said Dona Gracia.

"Yes, poor Aunt Lolly," said Francie.

"You must find it lonely," said Maria.

"Thank you, it's not so bad. You see, she gets up in the evening, and she knows a few people."

"Estoril is very good for the health," said Dona Gracia. "I always try to spend a few weeks here with my children, after a season in town."

"That must be very nice," said Francie.

So it went on, each female contributing her remark in turn. Through it all, Ruy said nothing. He must be bored to death, Francie thought, though he gave no sign of boredom.

But at last Maria, after an apology, broke off and spoke rapidly in Portuguese to her mother, then turned back to Francie with an explanation. "We can take a walk, if you like," she said. "It's pleasant now in the cool. Maman wishes to see a cousin here, and you and Ruy and I will go out for a little. Or don't you care to walk? We might drive instead."

"I'd love to walk," said Francie.

"Good," said Ruy, opening his mouth for the first time that evening.

Out of the hotel, the young people relaxed a little and the talk between the girls became animated again. Maria wanted to tell Francie about New York and the plays she had seen, and the shops and museums. She admired America, she said, passionately. American buildings were modern and beautiful, American boys were so polite in their way, American girls were so chic—"Like you, you know," she said earnestly. "You have a special style. It is a little *outré*, not too much, but something quite remarkable."

"Oh, you're too nice!" Francie blushed, and turned to Ruy. "And what about you in the States?" she asked. He was walking along silently, with a withdrawn expression on his face; she didn't know if he had been listening or not. "Do you like America as much as your sister does?" she asked.

"Oh, not as much," he said in cool tones. "Unlike Maria, I prefer my own country. But there are admirable things about New York, certainly. Yes."

Francie felt somewhat piqued. It wasn't that she wanted him to rave, she told herself, but he needn't act quite so kindly about liking New York—as if he were a dear old uncle patting her on the head. "Thank you very much," she said dryly.

Ruy laughed, and she decided to like him after all.

They strolled slowly along. At Francie's suggestion they turned off the main road in order to investigate shop windows along a side street.

"I like window-shopping," she said, "but I don't know where to go to see really nice things. Are there any interesting shops in Estoril?"

"If you mean dresses and hats, we haven't any places like yours," said Maria. "But one day we might go into Lisbon and look around, if you would care to do it."

"I'd like that," said Francie. "Tell me, Maria, what do you do all day? Have you a job, or do you just poke around the way everyone does I've met so far, playing games?"

She saw Ruy look at her in surprise, as Maria said, "Oh no, I haven't a job. Maman wouldn't allow it. That is the trouble here, you know; there isn't much for a girl to do."

"What about the boys?"

"Well, of course Ruy works. He helps my father," said Maria. "Ruy works very hard, don't you, Ruy?"

"Very," he said solemnly.

"No, I am not laughing. Please, Ruy, be serious," said Maria. "He really does, Francesca; I'm afraid he will make himself ill in this hot weather."

"My dear sister! For the past week I have done nothing but carry Maman's knitting bag from one place on the beach to another."

Maria said, "But this is your holiday. Wait until Papa gets back! Then Francesca will be surprised at your energy."

"Ah, that!" said Ruy.

Really, thought Francie, they were both very attractive young people. She felt much better already about Portugal.

It seemed that their father, Dom Rodrigo, was in the cork business (though Francie felt that with a name like that he ought to have been something more thrilling—a buccaneer, perhaps) and once every few years he went to the Western Hemisphere to discuss and arrange for the export of his cork. Ruy had been twice to Brazil, and he and Maria had both spent several months with their mother in the United States.

Dona Gracia had not enjoyed the adventure as much as her daughter had, said Maria. "Unless my Maman is with her sisters and cousins she is bored," she said, "but I loved it. I could find my way with my eyes covered, I think, from our apartment on Lexington Avenue to Carnegie Hall. It makes my heart jump when I hear people talking American."

Ruy looked scornful. Clearly it would take lots more than that to make his heart jump. "The Metropolitan Museum is good," he said in the tone of one making an admission.

This started Francie on the subject of her New York school, which was within easy distance of the museums. Ruy listened with more attention than he had hitherto shown. "You are an art student, then?" he asked.

"I was. I hope I shall be again." Francie's face fell as she remembered her current troubles. Maria's sympathetic questions drew her out; she talked until the whole story was disclosed.

"It is unfortunate," said Ruy at the end, "but I cannot understand why you feel everything is at an end."

"I don't," protested Francie. "I've been very careful not to get all tragic about it. Only I'm in a hurry, naturally, and I hate putting everything off."

"You could work by yourself."

"Oh, I know that," said Francie. "Of course I do sketch. At least I've been thinking about it lately. But I like help. I don't like going ahead on my own without advice."

Maria broke in, "Ruy, you are naughty. Don't listen to him, Francesca, until he stops teasing you. He knows how to help you. He's holding off and teasing."

"I am not sure," said Ruy to his sister, seriously. "There is no telling if she would suit Fontoura, or if Fontoura would suit her. We must go slowly. And at this moment there is no possible vacancy, of that I am sure."

"Do please tell me what you both mean," said Francie.

"Ruy is a painter," said Maria.

Ruy shook his head. "I play with paints."

"He is very clever, truly, and he attends a class in

painting, in Lisbon, which might be just what you want, Francesca," said Maria.

"You do, Ruy? How wonderful! Then you mean to be an artist, too?"

Ruy shrugged, and Maria replied for him. "My father didn't want him to be only a painter, nothing else. You see Ruy is his only son, and someone must go into the business from the family. And so he has given up his painting, except as a pastime." She hesitated, glancing shyly at her brother's frowning face. "He does not like me to talk about it, but he felt very bad."

Francie cried, "It was wrong! I do think it was wrong."

Ruy shrugged again. "It was not wrong. Had I been a true artist I would have thought it wrong, yes. Had I been a true artist I would have defied my father. But I was not good enough and I did not defy him, and he was not wrong." He smiled at Francie. "You are romantic, and so this shocks you."

Francie did not like being called romantic, but she could think of nothing to say.

"But Ruy, you will take Francesca to the class, will you not?" asked Maria.

"If she wishes," said Ruy, "and if Fontoura wishes. We can take our time, and think it over. There is no room as yet." He paused as another thought occurred to him.

"The fees are very high," he said. "I don't know if . . ."

"Oh, that doesn't matter," said Francie airily. "*That's* the least of my worries."

The da Souzas looked at each other with raised eyebrows.

CHAPTER 3

LAUGHTER rang out from the group gathered around a gay canvas swing on the veranda. "You'd never have the cheek!" cried a girl. "You know you wouldn't, Derek!"

"Oh, but I have," said a boy. "I warned you—"

They looked pretty, reflected Francie. They looked like somebody's romantic dream of life in a holiday place such as the Riviera or the Caribbean, one of those places she had never visited. The sun-tanned girls in their light clothes, the boys so clean and nice-looking, even the pretty French girl, spoke English with English accents. Nor was this odd, considering that most of them were English. Some of them belonged to families in the wine trade, families that had lived for two or three generations in Portugal, going back and forth between Oporto and "home."

Francie had discovered that these transplanted English had a local joke: those who lived in Oporto in the vineyard country, as the wine families of course did, pretended to look down on the permanent British residents of Lisbon. Many were the arguments about North versus South. But here in Estoril, the holiday place, such differences were forgotten.

And they were never real differences, reflected Francie. The Portuguese British all stuck together. They were like a family living abroad, a family that managed in spite of inevitable expansion and dilution to remember its relationship, and present a united front to the world. They were a tight little group. Everyone seemed to know everyone else, so that it gave Francie a slight twinge of envy to hear them laughing and talking of absent friends, of Bobby This and Brenda That. In just such a way, she thought wistfully, Glenn and Ruth and the others in Jefferson were probably speaking of her, to the utter mystification of some unlucky visitor who had never heard of Francie Nelson. It was good to belong somewhere, she said to herself, and felt homesick for her own friends.

Indoors the older people played bridge or canasta. She could see them through the glass, cozy and cut off from the noise and chatter of their young people. Aunt Lolly was there; she had actually ventured to spend several hours out of her room, and that was a good sign. Everyone but the family who lived in the villa was strange to both the Americans, but how easily she got on with strangers! From the bottom of her heart, Francie envied her godmother her calm assurance.

She herself was in the throes of shyness. She felt very much out of everything. Phyllis Wilkinson, the daughter of the house, was a nice girl. Francie had already met her several times, but Phyllis was newly engaged, and the presence of her young man had made her forget Francie for the moment. So Francie sat tongue-tied on the veranda, dutifully smiling when the others laughed, though the witticisms meant nothing to her. She would have liked to sparkle, but didn't know how to begin.

"I do feel like a drip," she thought despondently. "I wish I were spending the afternoon with Maria and Ruy. They're much more friendly."

She felt herself slipping back to the paralyzing timidity of her first days in England. But just before she despaired, Phyllis remembered the stranger.

"We'll have to see what kind of tennis Francie plays," she told the others. "I should think she's rather good. I've already seen her style at golf."

"Don't expect too much," said Francie. "Tennis isn't my game, really."

"What is, then?" asked Edward, a dark boy who

had been showing signs of wanting to talk to her. Francie said she liked swimming and spent a good deal of time on the hotel beach.

"I swim out of hours," she added, "during the siesta. As a matter of fact, I swim out of season, too. Nobody else seems to go in. At first I actually thought swimming wasn't allowed in Portugal except in midsummer."

The others laughed. "People think it's too cold," explained Phyllis. "Most Portuguese won't go into the water in the winter, but some other people are hardier. You'll see masses of people at Cascaes the year round, including the ex-crowned heads of Europe."

"Wearing everything to bathe in, even their crowns," put in another girl and everyone laughed again. Francie had to ask what the point was.

"We mean bathing suits," said Phyllis. "You see, the Portuguese police are awfully particular about costumes. I do hope you haven't been sporting a smart two-piece, or exposing your midriff or anything like that, because it isn't permitted. In the season, the police send picked men to patrol the beaches and protect public morals."

"We've heard sinister rumors that an unfortunate American female was taken away and never heard of again," said a red-haired girl, "because she wore a Bikini."

"A Bikini!" said Phyllis in horror. "There's no

doubt about it then. She must have been executed within twenty-four hours."

"No, but really, what are the rules?" asked Francie. "I've never got them straight."

They explained, all at once. One must wear a modest one-piece suit at the very least, and with shoulder straps. Even men had to wear tops to their trunks. "And that reminds me," said the dark boy, breaking off in the middle of a remark, "hadn't somebody better warn Mark about it? He's due to arrive soon, isn't he, Derek? Better drop him a line about our bathing suit restrictions. He'll bring ordinary trunks otherwise."

At the name Mark Francie pricked up her ears. She knew a Mark in England. But after all, she reminded herself, it was a common name. It would be silly to ask if this was the same boy. Nevertheless she listened alertly, and at last she was rewarded.

"Isn't that just like old Turnbull!" said one of the boys indulgently, after an anecdote.

Mark Turnbull! That was the name of her friend. Francie spoke up and asked where their Mark came from. Sure enough, Edward had known him at Oxford, where Mark had been when Francie left England. There were exclamations, and excited plans were made to arrange a meeting as soon as he should arrive. Francie started home in a happy whirl.

"Whatever do you think?" she demanded of Mrs.

Barclay in the car. "Mark Turnbull's coming to Lisbon! He's in Oporto already. Isn't that the queerest thing, to run into him here?"

"I can hardly agree, dear, until you tell me more about him. Who is Mark Turnbull? Is it that nice boy from Jefferson?"

Francie said, "Oh, Aunt Lolly, surely you remember? Oh—no, I don't suppose you do. I knew Mark in England. It's Glenn you're thinking about in Jefferson. I only wish he'd come too." She sighed a little. "But Mark, oh, Mark's *cute*. He's a dreamboat."

"What is the dreamboat doing in Portugal?" asked Aunt Lolly.

"I couldn't quite make out, but I gather he's got something or other to do with spinning mills in Manchester. Anyway, his father has. He's combining research into cloth design, or whatever it is—textiles, I guess you'd call it—with just plain visiting. The thing is, he's got these friends in Oporto he can stay with. People can't get out of England, you know, unless they've got business abroad. It's something to do with not being allowed any money."

"Yes, I know," said Aunt Lolly.

"It must be terrible, having to do without money when you're traveling," said Francie thoughtfully. "The poor English."

Her mind soon strayed from these unfamiliar paths,

[42]

for it seldom occurred to Francie that money troubles might exist. Pop always let her have whatever she needed. She went off into a pleasant reverie in which the past, when she had been a schoolgirl with a bit of a crush on Mark, mingled with a future in which matters were reversed and Mark was hopelessly enamored of her.

"He seemed so grown up when I first met him at Jennifer's," she said happily, coming out of it, "but now I think I could manage him. Did I ever tell you what happened, Aunt Lolly? You see there were these two boys, Mark and Peter, and they used to drop in at Jennifer's house where I was visiting. Jennifer was catty. I hated her. I'd never have gone to visit her, but Pop made me on account of Jennifer's father being in his company. Well, Jennifer liked Mark, so I made Mark like me." She looked doubtfully at Mrs. Barclay to see how she was taking this confession. "Of course we were very young," she added.

"What a nasty little beast you must have been," said Mrs. Barclay.

"I suppose I wasn't very nice," said Francie. "Not all the time, at any rate."

The car slowed to a gentle stop before the hotel door. It was growing dark. Aunt Lolly struggled to her feet, and with the help of the chauffeur and Francie got out and adjusted her cane. Francie walked with her to the elevator.

"I think I'll leave you here, Aunt Lolly," she said. "I'm going to take a little walk, a quick one before dinner."

Mrs. Barclay thought a moment. "Do you think you should, dear?" she asked.

"Why not?"

"Well, it's not customary, you know," said Mrs. Barclay.

"Oh, Aunt Lolly," said Francie impatiently. "A little walk! What's the harm in that?"

"No harm at all," said Aunt Lolly, "but it's not the custom. I know what you're going to say—that you needn't stick to the custom because you're a foreigner. But this time I think it might be unwise to go out alone. It's almost dark now, and I'm not sure it's safe."

Francie's lower lip thrust out. "I'm not afraid," she said.

"Very well, my dear. I'll see you later." Mrs. Barclay, with no sign of displeasure, stepped into the elevator and was whisked away.

Francie did not feel quite comfortable about it. Not that Aunt Lolly would brood about her or disapprove of things without saying so—you could trust her to be forthright. But it was barely possible that she was right, and that Francie was unwise to insist on having her own way.

"I just can't keep worrying about what strangers

might think or say about me," she decided at last. "Everyone's got to be a little independent in this world."

Now that she had made her point and was outside, however, she was not very much tempted to take her walk after all. It was difficult to decide where to go. Along the beach? No, there were too many barriers there. You could hardly walk at all before you ran into some private estate, and it was very dark below the street level. Inland, away from the shore altogether? Francie made a tentative beginning, crossing the wide street. But the roads which were so broad and open in the daytime, curving in the glaring sun between lawns, looked like canyons at night, for every house and garden had a wall, and every wall shed a shadow. The great trees along the roadside were sinister.

Francie settled at last for the ordinary stroll along the front. It was reasonably well lighted, so she recrossed the street. She stepped out briskly, and enjoyed it. The pedestrians at night weren't at all the same crowd that she was used to in the daytime. They were men, for the most part, sauntering in groups and talking pleasantly among themselves. Most of them looked like bank clerks in their conventional dark clothes and white shirts. A family, complete with all the children down to the smallest toddler, moved along in a shifting mass. As they passed, Mama and the older girls looked curiously at Francie, and she looked as curiously back. The men pretended not to see her. One very small girl in a long pink frock, her hair pulled up to a smooth glistening knot at the top of her head, stopped in Francie's path and stared up at her with enormous black eyes. She was exactly like a Kate Greenaway child, thought Francie.

"You darling!" she said impulsively, and leaned down. The child was startled and skittered back to her family, and everyone laughed. Francie heard them chattering behind her as she went on.

A peasant girl came along, carrying a large bundle on her head. Her full skirts swished, her bare feet made no noise on the pavement. Three ragged small boys followed Francie for a little, holding out their palms and begging. She gave them some coins and they disappeared.

The sea was lost now in black distance, except when a car turned out of a side road and threw its lights across the beach. Even here by an oil-soaked highway, the air was fragrant with sea smell and some kind of flower perfume.

"I must get out into the country somehow, for a long visit," thought Francie. "I'm wasting my time. I *must* see more of Portugal. I wonder if the da Souzas could help me."

Ahead of her she saw a familiar figure approaching.

At first she thought her imagination was playing tricks on her, but as he reached the light of the street-lamp she saw that it was indeed Ruy da Souza.

"Ruy!" she cried in pleased tones.

Ruy paused, startled. His eyes went beyond Francie, as if he were looking for a companion. "Good evening," he said. "Are you—is everything all right?"

"Perfectly all right, thank you," said Francie. "Are you going back to the hotel?"

He seemed to think it over. What was the matter with him, she wondered irritably. Surely he knew if he was or wasn't going to the hotel!

"Anyway, I am," she said, turning round. "I came out for a walk, but I'd better hurry now, or Aunt Lolly will be worried."

Ruy fell into step with her. "Worried? She does not know you are out so late, then," he said. His tone implied that this explained everything.

"Oh yes she does," said Francie blithely. Again Ruy looked puzzled, or at least uncertain.

He was in an uncommunicative mood, and replied to all her remarks with monosyllables. When they arrived at the door he hesitated.

"Aren't you coming in?" Francie asked in surprise.

Ruy shrugged, and walked in behind her. Across the lobby Francie saw Maria and Dona Gracia, evidently waiting for him. They looked surprised at sight of her, and Dona Gracia did not seem pleased, for some reason.

"Moody people, these Portuguese," thought Francie as she rang for the elevator. "You never know where you are with them."

CHAPTER 4

THE sea breathed softly against pale sand, and the air was gentle as milk. Mrs. Barclay was reading in bed; her curtains had actually been drawn back enough to let the light in. ("It's growing cooler now," the chambermaid said in explanation.) Francie sat near the bed, sharing her breakfast.

In the Paris edition of the *Herald Tribune* which Aunt Lolly had just handed over across the coffeepot, Francie read incredulously of the cold weather at home. Snow-bound cars in Chicago held up for days in their parking lots, fires from overstoked furnaces, floods where ice dams had broken. She looked around her at the warm, sunny room and asked herself, "Is it the same world?"

There was a knock on the door, and the maid brought in the morning mail. Francie eagerly tore

[49]

open a letter with an American stamp, and Mrs. Barclay, looking up from her own letters, saw the girl's contented expression change as she read.

"Anything wrong?" asked Aunt Lolly.

"Nothing really," said Francie, "but I'm getting peeved at Ruth. This letter's from her."

Aunt Lolly said, "Let me think—oh yes, Ruth's your great friend in Jefferson, isn't she?"

"That's the one. We've been intimate friends all our lives." Francie propped her chin on her hands. "Aunt Lolly, do you think I'm getting boastful lately? You know—stuck up?"

"Boastful?" Aunt Lolly paused a moment to think gravely about her reply. "No, I really hadn't noticed it. Why? Is Ruth accusing you of it?"

"In a roundabout way she is. At least that's what I think she means. Listen to this—" Francie picked up the letter and read aloud, " 'I'd ask you heaps more, only I'm sure you're getting much too grand to bother answering the questions of us ordinary people.' Now I ask you, is that fair, Aunt Lolly? I'm always writing to Ruth. I'm always answering her. I'll bet I write more often than she does, even."

Her voice trembled. She was hurt more deeply than she could have explained, and more deeply really than the silly little sentence warranted. Francie was in a sensitive mood. Recent developments in Portugal were more to blame for this than was Ruth.

"She's probably joking," came Aunt Lolly's calm voice in the midst of her struggle against tears. If Aunt Lolly noticed any agitation, she was tactfully ignoring it.

Francie recovered herself. "I *haven't* been boasting," she said.

"Then I shouldn't worry. Ruth may be a tiny bit jealous of your visit to Europe. It would be only natural, wouldn't it? If I were you I'd ignore it, and write to her as usual, as if she hadn't said anything spiteful."

"Oh dear, everything seems to get difficult all at once," said Francie. "I didn't mean that really," she added hastily. "I only meant I feel strange here, with all these new people, and now here's Ruth telling me I'm acting strange with her, too."

Aunt Lolly waited, but Francie did not continue with the subject. There was a silence, while Mrs. Barclay returned to her mail and Francie to the *Herald Tribune*. At last Mrs. Barclay put down her papers and took off her glasses. "There are times," she said carefully, "when we don't like anybody very much, and it seems as if nobody likes us very much either. Yes, my dear, I have those days, too. Just try to remember that we can't be everything everybody wants us to be, *all* the time. It would be superhuman."

Francie kissed her and went to her own room. Aunt Lolly was wonderful, of course. "But she can't know quite how I feel," Francie thought, "because she's never felt like a fool when she's with foreigners."

Uneasily she thought again of the afternoon she had spent, the day before, with the da Souza family. It was a week since her walk alone in the dark near the hotel, when she had seen, or fancied she had seen, a coldness in Dona Gracia's face at the sight of her coming in with Ruy. Nobody had ever spoken about it, not even Maria. It had evidently blown over. The da Souzas had no doubt reminded themselves that American girls have a different code of behavior, as they had seen in New York.

So everything was all right again until Dom Rodrigo came home and the da Souza family left the hotel to move back to their flat in Lisbon. Francie missed them. Maria still kept in close touch with her—after all, Estoril was practically part of the city, only a short train ride off—but still, Francie didn't see as much of Maria now, and Ruy was busy with his father at the office. Francie told herself it was all for the best. She had been neglecting her English acquaintances in her eagerness to learn more about Portugal, and this made it rather awkward for Aunt Lolly sometimes. Now she was able to spend more time with Phyllis and the other young English people. Then yesterday she had seen all the da Souzas together, and it hadn't been a success.

"I'll write to Penny," she suddenly resolved. It

would take her mind off her uneasiness. She would tell Penny funny little things that would amuse her. Penny, her English friend, was studying drama production in New York, on a scholarship.

Once started on the letter, Francie forgot the time. Her pen raced on as she touched lightly on one harmless frivolity after another. There had been an evening's marvelous dancing, she said, at the Casino, where she had gone with Phyllis, Derek and David. She had worn a long dress, blue net over pink, which was dreamy.

"On Sunday afternoon we went to the beach at Cascaes, six of us. Cascaes is the most fashionable place to bathe. You can guess how fashionable when I tell you I bagged two kings in one hour, unless you want to argue (as David did) that Don Jaime isn't a genuine king, but only a pretender. We collect royalties; it's like playing Beaver. There are so many kings and queens around here that I hardly notice them any more."

Francie paused, doubtful for a minute as she thought of Jefferson's comments if she had written like this to anyone there. But Penny would understand and laugh with her.

"The same day, later on, we went to a place called Machado's, which you'd love. We went to hear the *fado* because it's supposed to be especially good there, and I hadn't heard any. Machado's is a little café, not at all posh, and I was crazy about it. There are paintings on the wall, up under the ceiling—portraits of popular bullfighters and *fado* singers. Ruy da Souza once told me bullfighting and *fado* always go together, the people are so fond of them both.

"In case you haven't figured it out for yourself, the word means 'fate' literally, but actually it's a particular kind of folk song. I always used to think of folk songs as jolly tunes, but it seems I was quite wrong. Ruy says they are sad, usually—all folk songs, I mean. There's no 'usually' about *fado*, which is always sad, and pretty much the same all the time, a long, wailing, droning tune with words that simply drool. Every time I ask anybody to translate one it turns out to be something like, 'I'm a poor young man and I haven't enough to eat, and I'm hopelessly in love with the girl across the street.' Only I'm afraid even that's too sensible to be typical. Ruy says—"

Here Francie paused thoughtfully, then scratched out the last two words and started a fresh paragraph.

"The da Souzas have left Estoril and gone back to town. Maria took me home yesterday and I had tea with them," she wrote. She paused again, looking rather blankly out of the window.

It wasn't any use, trying to put everything down in a letter. It would take too long and Penny might be bored. "I'll tell her all about it when I see her," Francie decided at last. She went on sitting at the desk, nevertheless, thinking of the letter she might have written.

It had been a queer afternoon with the da Souzas. Francie was eager to see Dom Rodrigo, after having heard so much about him. She had a feeling that his children were rather in awe of him, and when she met him she could understand why this was so. Dom Rodrigo looked like an older Ruy, but he was not as willowy as his son, and his facial expression was very different. Ruy looked severe sometimes, and imperturbable, but Dom Rodrigo actually seemed fierce.

He wasn't fierce in his speech, however. He was polite to Francie—not charming, but perfectly polite. "I'll bet he has a terrible temper, though, when he thinks it's necessary," she thought. They had all been like wooden dolls, sitting upright in the tall, cool drawing room, sipping at their tea and eating one cake apiece. All the ease Francie had formerly felt with the young people was gone. Dom Rodrigo talked about the parks of New York, and Long Island. He asked about Francie's father. Francie thought there was a shade of unbending in his manner when she told him the position Pop held in the company. He asked Francie if she had been to Paris, and Rome, and Madrid, and he told her something about these places. It was all very courteous and chilly.

Dona Gracia had not joined in the talk, but confined her remarks to purely utilitarian matters. "Maria, ring the bell for more hot water," she said, and "Do take a little honey."

Francie came home with a general impression that everyone had behaved most properly, and that nothing at all had been done or said that mattered in the slightest. She felt frozen out of Portugal.

"It was very nice," she wrote, "and of course I was interested because it was the first time I had ever seen a Portuguese home. It was beautifully furnished, with lovely sharp accents of black and white and gleaming dark wood, and in the most exquisite order. But I think Ruy and Maria are more fun when they're on their own."

She might have added, but didn't, that she had felt a heavy atmosphere of disapproval in the air— disapproval of herself. "I don't know why Dom Rodrigo should think I'm so awful," thought Francie mournfully, "but I'm sure he does."

She was equally sure she would not see very much more of Ruy and Maria. "I suppose Dom Rodrigo's old-fashioned and doesn't like American ways," she decided. "It must be true, what Phyllis told me—the Portuguese don't really open up to foreigners. They're too formal."

Well, it was a pity, but it couldn't be helped. And certainly it couldn't be put into a letter, even to an understanding friend like Penny. Penny would laugh at her for being sensitive. Francie was just bringing the letter to a close when the telephone rang. It was Maria.

"I have just been thinking," said Maria, in her ordinary friendly manner, "about the promise we made to take you shopping. Unfortunately, Ruy cannot come, but my mother would be glad to take us around this afternoon, if you have no other plans. All right? Good. We shall meet you at the station, as usual. At four o'clock."

So much for her imaginary troubles, thought light-hearted Francie as she sealed the letter. Miraculously, Dom Rodrigo had ceased to be an ogre. He was merely formal, that was all. It was a different manner than she was used to, but it didn't mean unfriendliness.

That afternoon they started out in the banking quarter of the city, because the jewelry shops, according to Dona Gracia, were the most amusing for foreigners. Francie went delightedly from one window to another, fascinated by the many little objects in gold and silver filigree.

"Do look at that little cart and bull, Maria," she said. "Look, it's got a barrel on it!"

"Yes, that is supposed to be wine," said Maria. "See, that silver ship is carrying barrels, too."

Francie went to the next window, where she fell into raptures over the necklaces displayed there, and the little silver-gilt caravels. "But I suppose this must bore you, Dona Gracia," she said. "It is always the same, I suppose, for people who live here. You must be awfully tired of filigree."

"It is pretty," said Dona Gracia indulgently. "Now what else would you like to see?"

Francie thought it over. "Do you need to do any shopping for the house?" she asked. "I mean groceries or anything like that? I'd like to see the way food is sold here."

"Yes, that is always interesting," said Maria, and Dona Gracia seemed pleased. She did have a few housekeeping errands, she admitted, and Francie was welcome to come along if she liked. So off they went to the provision shop, and Francie wandered about among sausages and great barrels of rice and tins of olive oil, sniffing and peering, until Dona Gracia had finished her shopping.

"Now," said Maria, "we can show you the clothes shops. But you must remember, we don't buy our dresses already made. You'll only see cloth on sale, and perhaps some pretty embroidery."

They were not far from the grocer's, off the main street, when Francie saw a wide-open door into a shop where glimpses of the stock made her curious. She asked Maria to step inside with her for a look around. Maria hesitated. "It's nothing very interesting," she said. "Only the kind of cotton that our poorer people buy for their clothes, and rough blankets and rugs. Still, if you would like—" She looked inquiringly at her mother, who nodded.

Francie made her way to the bolts of material on the counter, whose brilliant colors caught her eye. "They're lovely," she said. "They're the prettiest things I've seen here. Look, this is almost like paisley. Don't you like them, Maria?"

"Oh yes, I like them," said Maria, "but they are very coarse material, you know—harsh and thick."

"But the patterns!"

"They are very pretty," agreed Dona Gracia. "I use them myself sometimes. Not for clothes, of course"—Francie smiled at the idea of the quietly elegant Dona Gracia in such gay, intricate designs— "but for cushion covers in a country house. Even, sometimes, for curtains. They are not bad at all."

"They are beautiful," Francie insisted. She felt strongly drawn to the patterns; she would have liked to buy some. But Maria was so patronizing about them that she resolved to come back alone some other day and examine them further. For the time being, she contented herself with a short tour of more conventional places. She bought nylons and a few lace handkerchiefs in a French shop. The handkerchiefs were expensive. Dona Gracia looked surprised that Francie had so much money with her.

Francie came back to Estoril smiling. "It was terribly interesting. I wish you could have come along," she reported to Mrs. Barclay. "The peasant things were best. You and I will have to go to that handicraft museum as soon as you're better. Dona Gracia says that's where they have all the best products from everywhere—embroidery and weaving and so forth, arranged according to the district that specializes in it. I wish this hotel would use the lovely stripy stuff I saw instead of this tiresome chintz. It is almost like our Navaho blankets, but the colors are more delicate. Oh, and then we had tea at that place Maria likes so much, where you can get ice-cream sodas. Ruy met us there. I asked him again about his art school and he says he'll take me to see the teacher."

"And did Dom Rodrigo meet you, too?" asked Mrs. Barclay.

"Goodness, no. He wouldn't have time for such frivolity, I shouldn't think," said Francie. "Everybody else in the family turned up sooner or later, though. At least it looked like it. Relatives kept stopping at our table to talk to Dona Gracia, and it was all lots of fun."

She went off humming to take her bath.

CHAPTER 5

I WOULDN'T have known you," said Mark.

Francie grimaced at him. "I don't quite know how to take that," she said.

"Changed, has she?" asked Mr. Wilkinson, their host.

"The last time I saw her, sir," said Mark," she was a scruffy little schoolgirl with a hockey stick in her hand."

"And now look at her," said Derek. "Quite a change."

"Mark Turnbull, you know that's not true!" cried Francie. "I wasn't scruffy, and you never saw me playing hockey in your life. I don't see how you can tell such whoppers."

Mark insisted that she had been frightfully scruffy,

and continued to talk like an indulgent uncle until Francie turned the tables on him, and told a few hastily fabricated stories of her own about his habits as an Oxford undergraduate. Then Mark behaved himself.

Even if it had been true, if she had changed very much, reflected Francie—but of course that was only Mark's nonsense—*he* most certainly hadn't. He brought with him such an atmosphere of England that it was a shock to look around the large, cool rooms and remember that now they were both in Portugal. And how easily one slipped back into the old moods! Francie almost laughed aloud, recalling her scorn of that particular kind of boy-and-girl teasing when she first heard it going on between Mark and Jennifer at the Tennisons' country home. Kindergarten stuff, she had called it, when the boys pulled Jennifer's hair, and she had pretended to be furious.

"Now I'm doing it myself," Francie thought. "And Mark really is cute. He always was, of course." She sighed. "He's not quite the answer to a maiden's prayer I used to think, all the same," she warned herself. "It was my state of mind that made him look so wonderful. In those days I was just naturally starved for dates. And then, of course, Jennifer wanted him . . ."

In England she had been crammed back into childhood like an oversized genie in a very small bottle.

It was different now. Dates were once more a commonplace, thank goodness. And so they should be, she thought, for any right-minded, right-living American girl.

"Seriously," said Mark, under cover of the dinner-table talk, "you've come on quite a bit, Francie. I mean to say, you have, you know. Putting all joking aside."

"Is that good?" she asked cheerfully. Not accustomed to the phrase, he gaped at her. She altered it to, "Changed, I mean, for better or for worse?"

Mark hesitated. "I'd want notice on that question," he said at last, and turned to his other partner.

On the whole, she thought she knew the answer. Her self-confidence, which had been taking a beating lately, began to revive. Good old Mark for appreciating her! Familiar old Mark! Nice old Mark, pulling her leg the way he'd done in the old days. It all made her feel quite travel-worn and world-weary, but it was enjoyable. She hoped he would have to stay in Lisbon a good long time.

"That depends on my company," said Mark when she asked him what his plans were. "Officially I'm on a job up north near Oporto, and I daresay they'll be telling me soon to report there again. But at present my old man has told me to stay here, in touch with some of the Portuguese chaps who are working with us. You ought to come north yourself, you know.

You can't say you've seen Portugal unless you've visited Oporto. We'll give you a good time. Lisbon's very well, but there are other places."

"I know. I do want to get around," said Francie. "I don't do too badly as it is, though, considering Mrs. Barclay's laid up so much of the time."

"I rather expected to find you all entangled with the American colony."

"There aren't so many of them in my age group. Aunt Lolly goes to their lunches and so forth, but there's a shortage of young people. I see more of *these*." She nodded toward her friends at the table. "We golf a little and we play tennis at Cascaes or the Casino. You'll like the courts here—they're super. But after all I'm in a foreign country. I'm trying to do more things I wouldn't be doing at home."

"Well, yes," said Mark rather doubtfully, "but you don't want to overdo it."

"You can't overdo it," said Francie.

Mark said, "Oh, come now. You mean to say you want to go native and all that?"

"I don't know what you mean."

"You wouldn't want to be a Portuguese girl really," he said, "with chaperones following you wherever you go. That wouldn't suit your style at all."

"It most decidedly would not," put in Phyllis, overhearing their talk. "Francie's the very opposite of Portuguese. She goes around all alone in the most

[64]

independent manner, at all times of the day and night."

She spoke in a spirit of good-natured raillery, but Mark took it seriously. "Is that true?" he asked Francie.

"Why shouldn't I? The conventions here are simply ridiculous," said Francie. "I think it's just silly trying to live up to them. After all, I'm American. It's not the way I was brought up. Why be hypocritical?" She paused, but as Mark still looked unconvinced she added, "Phyllis is getting at me just because I went to the movies by myself the other afternoon and she happened to meet me coming out."

Phyllis laughed. "Happened to meet her! The awed populace did everything to call my attention. They even cleared a space for her. There was no chance of missing Francie in that crowd. It was after dark," she said in explanation.

"It's quite all right really," Francie assured Mark, who was frowning. "Nothing ever happens to me."

"No, of course not, and I don't suppose anything will," he said. "They're a law-abiding people on the whole. But you don't want to overdo it. I'm not thinking of danger, but it just doesn't look well."

"Oh, pooh," said Francie.

Maria and Ruy had taken Francie to her first bullfight, to watch a celebrated matador making his first appearance of the season. It was seven o'clock on Sunday evening when they brought her back to Estoril, and they came in for a farewell cup of coffee. Aunt Lolly was waiting. The hotel lounge was brilliant, crowded with holiday-makers. Motorists or residents, they were gaily dressed and having fun in their decorous way. There was never anything Sundaylike, as Francie knew it, on that day of the week in Portugal.

"What was it like?" asked Mrs. Barclay, after they had ordered their coffee and cakes.

Francie said, "Well . . . I feel all mixed up."

"She really is mixed up," Maria assured Mrs. Barclay. "She was torn two ways, all through the show."

"I was afraid she might faint," said Ruy gravely. "English ladies do now and then. I cannot understand why they come to see it in the first place."

Francie said, "I wasn't near fainting, truly. It didn't seem that bad. The pageantry was marvelous! I kept wishing Penny could be with us because she loves the theater in great gobs, and that is what a bullfight is. But—well, I don't know if I'd ever want to go again."

"If you were to go only once again," said Ruy, "you would become addicted."

"Then I won't," said Francie definitely. "Still, I had to see it once, to discover what all the talk is about. The thing is, you simply mustn't begin to think about the bull. I know I should simply hate a Spanish fight. They're much more cruel, with all the horses, and really killing the bull."

"So, now you have done your duty," said Ruy. "You have not come to Portugal in vain."

Francie looked at him suspiciously. She didn't know how serious he might be. "I think on the whole I'll go back to ballet," she said. "I can enjoy that with a clear conscience."

"Oh, how lucky you are! I would give anything," said Maria, "for a whole season of ballet in New York. Some day I can do it again, perhaps."

Mrs. Barclay said, "Let's hope you can visit Francie in New York soon, and have your fill of theater."

"It is my dream," said Maria.

Francie had been biding her time all afternoon, waiting to make a request of Ruy. Now the time seemed to have come. "Speaking of dreams, aren't you ever going to introduce me to Fontoura, or are you going to keep putting me off?" she demanded. She said in explanation to Aunt Lolly, "That's Ruy's friend with the art classes, you know. Ruy seems to think I'll snub him, or do something else perfectly terrible. He's afraid to take me to the school. Aren't you, Ruy?"

Ruy said carefully, "I don't think you'll snub him. It is rather the other way round. Fontoura is a serious man, who wishes his pupils to be serious as well."

"You mean I'm not serious!"

"I did not say that," said Ruy. "Only, forgive me,

it doesn't sound like the sort of pupil Fontoura is interested in—a rich American girl on a visit to Estoril." At sight of Francie's hurt face he added hurriedly, "That is because he doesn't know you. I will explain to him." He looked into her eyes and repeated emphatically, "I will explain to him, Francesca. *I* know you are serious."

"There!" Maria's voice dispersed Francie's embarrassment. "It is settled, if Ruy says he will do that. Fontoura will take his word for it."

The solemnity of the discussion rather depressed Francie. Of course it was sweet of Ruy to accept her good intentions—and he did seem to think she had talent as well, otherwise he would never consent to introduce her to his precious school. ("Though he may be keen on me. That would explain it," she admitted in her thoughts.) But about his promise there was an atmosphere of what might almost be called dedication.

"It needn't matter all that much," she reflected uneasily. "After all, Fontoura's studio is only an art school, when all's said and done. It's not a church."

Her misgivings were not allayed on the important day of days when Ruy arrived to escort her to the studio. When Francie thanked him for his trouble as they started out, he said formally,

"It is nothing. My father was glad to give me the

morning free. He sends his compliments to Miss Francesca."

"That was very kind of him," said Francie in rather faint tones.

She was silent as they walked toward the train platform. Her portfolio had never seemed so large and clumsy. She would not permit Ruy to carry it, though he offered to. Looking timidly at him, she saw to her surprise that he was smiling in a quiet way.

"You are nervous," he said at last, not asking a question but stating a fact. "I know what it is like, the first time. Never mind, Fontoura won't hurt you."

Francie forced a laugh. "He might hurt my feelings, though," she said.

Ruy did not deny it. Her nervousness increased. She tried to concentrate on the glimpses of sea which she caught as the train rolled along. A fleet of fishing boats was coming in. She saw little russet sails like a flight of ducks, and then they were out of sight, cut off by a great urban block of raspberry-colored flats.

"The sky is blue," she began to recite to herself, deliberately trying to forget her ordeal. "The ground is tan, with here and there a patch of tough vegetation. Olive trees, perhaps? The sky is blue; the sea is blue. The natives are good-looking people and the women walk with the straightest backs I have ever seen, and their full skirts are wonderfully graceful. Oh, dear, aren't we there yet? The sky is blue—"

[69]

"Courage," said Ruy. They had arrived at their station. He pushed open the door and stepped out in the casual European manner Francie could never get used to, for she came of a people that always rushed in and out of trains. Still, she followed him as casually as she could manage.

They were now in the outskirts of Lisbon, in a quarter that was less ancient than the squares and cathedrals Francie knew. They walked uphill along a wide thoroughfare, then turned off into a curving street, between stucco houses painted in a variety of soft colors—yellow, pastel blue and pink. The tints had weathered in the sun and looked, somehow, exactly right for the ground on which they stood.

"The Portuguese are the most amazing people, aren't they?" asked Francie. "It's as if they couldn't go wrong on houses, or streets, or any kind of city planning. Look there now, down that side street. Those places were built at different times, I suppose, just any old way, and yet they couldn't be righter. Or am I talking nonsense?"

"No, it is not nonsense," said Ruy. "It is our particular genius which you have recognized."

The strange streets twisted in a most confusing manner, but the young people turned in at last to a small cobbled lane which ended at a door set in a brick wall.

"It was a garage," explained Ruy, "and Fontoura discovered the possibilities accidentally. He was living in that house there, and happened to see that the light is not cut off from the garage roof." He rang the bell as if he were putting a full stop to the sentence, all too soon for Francie, who gripped her portfolio in a last-minute panic.

A servant answered the door, and went to call Fontoura. The much-heralded man was small, with a lined little face, clean shaven. He came rapidly into the anteroom, wearing a stained smock. At sight of Ruy his face brightened, and to Francie's secret amusement they greeted each other in the Portuguese manner to which she was not yet accustomed, with joyful exclamations and a half-embrace. There was quite a session on the threshold, what with introductions, compliments, and Ruy's interpretations between Fontoura and Francie. Talking, they walked together into the main workroom, a long, glass-roofed hall.

Francie sniffed. The odor was reminiscent—oil, turps, wet clay, the smell of all art schools anywhere in the world. In spite of being worried, she felt cheered. Five or six young people, in smocks or aprons, were working from a model down at the other end of the room. The model was a chunky young woman standing on a dais. Three of the students had easels, and the other three were sitting on the floor using sketch pads, Francie noticed. It seemed a very independent sort of class. She looked at them with bright, interested eyes, wondering if she would be joining their ranks soon, and they looked back in friendly curiosity.

Ruy had already notified Fontoura of their visit, she knew, and had overcome his objections to taking on another pupil, though at first the artist had insisted he was already too crowded. Everything depended now on what he thought of her work. Francie did not dare to wonder what might happen if he didn't consider her good enough. While he and Ruy talked, she wandered over to the wall and pretended to examine some charcoal drawings that were pinned there. She had already put down her portfolio on a little table.

A pause in the chatter behind her made her turn around. Horrors! Fontoura and Ruy had opened the portfolio and were looking through her things. She hurried back to them.

"You see what I mean," Ruy said to Fontoura, speaking English in deference to her feelings. "A good sense of color. The drawing, of course, needs—"

Fontoura cut in with a flood of Portuguese. "If only I'd learned something of this language before!" thought Francie. She listened intently, trying to make out what on earth he was saying, but it was impossible to tell. Ruy smiled at her apologetically, patiently waiting until Fontoura drew breath.

At last Fontoura turned to her, and said, "All right. You like to come tomorrow?"

It was as easy as that.

In a rush of relief, Francie swept through the business details like a whirlwind. Here again Ruy had to help in the interpreting. He explained that Fontoura did not run his school like a regular, formal institution; he was a private teacher only. But there were various classes in the studio, some of them not taught by himself. Francie could have her choice of several. There was one course in clay modeling, for instance. Fontoura believed that modeling was a help to any artist, even one who like Francie wished to specialize in painting. There was another in which a teacher took you to the Museum and helped you to make copies of masterpieces. The ordinary drawing Fontoura himself took care of. He also criticized water colors, and gave occasional demonstrations.

"Tell him I'd like to take all the courses I can fit in," said Francie.

"All?" Ruy looked surprised. "It is not the custom. Most people do only two or three."

"But I'm awfully keen," said Francie.

"But Francesca," said Ruy, "have you thought of what it will cost? Fontoura is not cheap, you know, and the other masters' courses, not to speak of your materials—"

Francie made an expansive gesture. "That's the least

of my worries," she said. "You tell him I'll take as much as the traffic will bear."

Fontoura too looked a little surprised, but he bowed and said, "Good."

"If he'll make out what it all costs, or ask his secretary to, I'll pay in advance," said Francie. "Pop likes me to pay in advance."

"Once a quarter is the custom," said Ruy, but Francie said she would pay a year's fees immediately.

She was so happy she wanted to skip on the way back to the station.

"I hope the arrangement will be satisfactory for everybody," said Ruy. "You are so impulsive, you Americans!"

"Oh, I do thank you, Ruy. I do appreciate what you've done," said Francie. "I can hardly wait for tomorrow."

CHAPTER 6

FRANCIE didn't get to school the next day after all. She felt the slightest bit guilty about it, but, as she told herself, it really wasn't her fault or anybody else's that Mrs. Barclay had made a date for her while she was out.

"Provisionally, of course," said Mrs. Barclay, in explanation. "I told Mark when he telephoned that I wasn't sure you wouldn't be busy, and it never occurred to me you'd be starting in on your classes so promptly. But you can explain to Mark; I've no doubt he'll understand."

Francie thought it over. Mark's invitation, which included Aunt Lolly, was for an all-day jaunt to Coruche, in the country east of Lisbon, a region famous for its bulls. There on ranches the tough little bulls were bred and trained in preparation for their appearance in the arenas of Spain and Portugal.

"What are we going to do?" she asked. "Just visit some ranch and look at the cows?"

"No, it's more than that, I believe," said Mrs. Barclay. "There's a ceremony called the *corrida*, the running, when the bulls are moved into Coruche. It seems they don't just move them; they make a party of it. The bulls are herded along the streets and everyone in town comes to watch. It must be interesting. Mark sounded most enthusiastic."

"Well . . . I must say it sounds awfully tempting. I guess school can wait one more day," Francie decided. "I don't feel quite right about starting in before I've paid the fees, anyway. Let's leave the arrangements as you made them." Besides, she told herself, it would be a pity to spoil Aunt Lolly's first all-day expedition, since she seemed to feel well enough to undertake it.

They started out in two cars about the middle of the morning, carrying a picnic lunch in a large hamper. The Wilkinsons, who had arranged the party, had of course invited Phyllis' young man Derek as well. There was the usual polite discussion, always necessary in Portugal, as to which car should go first and avoid the dust which the other must take.

The road was bad indeed, but it was the first time Francie had been well out in the countryside and she was fascinated. First they drove through a sparsely wooded, hilly country, between tall pines, but then the land flattened out and the woods were left behind. The road now meandered, leading them over country that looked to the Americans almost like desert.

"I do love these pretty little houses," said Mrs. Barclay as they drove past a farmhouse that gleamed with fresh whitewash. A broad band of turquoise blue ran around the building near its base, and the shutters were picked out with the same color. A similar blue band encircled the white wall that enclosed house and barn. "It's a beautiful color," she said. "Are all the houses in Portugal trimmed in the same way?"

Mrs. Wilkinson said, "No, it's just the preferred design in this district. You find other arrangements in the north. In the region near Oporto, for instance, they all go in for gray on white. And in other places they use black bands instead of the gray. It's most effective, I think."

Within a mile or two they saw another house. Francie said, "It's rather thickly settled, considering."

"Considering what?" asked Mark.

"Well, I can't figure out what the people do who live here," said Francie. "You can see for yourself, nobody's farming this land. It's all dry red soil. Nothing grows on it but those scrubby trees."

Mark slowed up and stopped the car. "I won't be

long, Mrs. Wilkinson," he said. "I'm going to show our American cousin here what the trees are."

He had paused near a very strange-looking tree with a naked pink trunk. The branches were brown and gnarled and appeared normal, but the trunk, as Francie saw at close quarters, had been totally stripped of its thick bark. "Whatever's happened to it?" she asked.

"That's a cork tree," said Mark. "Here's where a lot of the cork you use for bottles comes from. It's an important industry. It's what keeps the people busy, the ones you were worrying about, who live in those pretty houses. Sometimes they grow olives as well."

"Will this tree die now?"

"Oh no," said Mrs. Wilkinson. "It will grow more bark, and then in a few years they'll strip it again."

"Rather on the sheep-shearing principle, I always think," said Mark, starting up the car.

They had their lunch by the roadside and then drove on into the fringes of the town. A few gaily-colored ribbons had been stretched across the streets from window to window, and there were temporary archways covered with flowers, but the brightest splashes of color, in rugs and patterned shawls, hung like banners from the windows of the high, flat-fronted houses. Francie was thrilled with them.

"There, Aunt Lolly! Those are something like the

blankets and heavy rugs I saw in that store. Don't they look lovely in the sun? Look at that one with big roses."

Craning his neck to see what she was talking about, Mark nearly ran into a knot of people in the road. They shouted, but cheerfully. Nobody wanted to be angry on this day of festivity.

"Some of those patterns are jolly interesting," he admitted. "My father has sometimes thought of picking up ideas from the Portuguese weavers for our textiles. But on the whole, domestic English taste runs to quieter colors."

"I know. Floral patterns in pastel pink and blue," said Francie, in innocent tones.

"Well, what's the matter with good honest flowers?" Mark asked sharply. The shaft had struck home, but he grinned at the same time.

"Nothing at all, within limits," said Francie. "It's only that I get tired of flowery dresses, day after day."

Mark said, "We don't all want to look like pirates." He spoke with emphasis and looked pointedly at the brilliant red and blue bandanna Francie was wearing for a collar. It was an innovation of her own.

"Don't you like it?" she asked, rather disappointed.

"As a matter of fact, I do. It suits you. But you can carry it off, and lots of girls couldn't. It's not English style, actually. Remember, in textiles one tries to design for the average woman."

"I don't see why," said Francie. "I wouldn't if I were doing it."

Mark said, "We try out a few original patterns every season, of course, in the big multiple shops we supply. Once in a while a novelty catches on, but in general they're conservative in England."

"You're telling me!" said Francie, and they both laughed.

"If it comes to that," added Mark thoughtfully, "nobody's more conservative than these Portuguese in their taste. Don't think that merely because they're traditionally devoted to bright red or blue or black—" Here his lecture was broken off; a driving emergency had arisen, brought on by a large cart, ox-drawn and laden with big pieces of cork bark, coming along in the opposite direction.

"We'll simply have to leave the cars outside the town, Mark, because of these narrow roads," said Mrs. Wilkinson after they had got around the cart. "Let's see what the others are doing, and follow them."

A man in a black slouch hat told them where they should put the cars, and they came back on foot to the public square, where temporary wooden benches had been erected along the side of a little park. They squeezed in on the back bench, which was highest and safest. It was almost time for the running to begin, Phyllis told them, and the whole town was there.

Families with small children sought the safety of the bleacherlike benches, but the young men all stood around in the street, looking eagerly toward the end from which the bulls were expected.

Then, with a fanfare of horns, the local band came marching. Following them came a series of slow-moving oxcarts, some piled with bark and others with olive wood. "In celebration of local industry," Mrs. Wilkinson explained.

After that, there was rather a hiatus, filled only with the sound of low-voiced chatter and impatient babies crying. Then from the distance they heard excited shouting that drew rapidly nearer, and the bulls came in.

They looked small and frightened. They seemed hardly more than calves, mere pygmies compared with the great oxen that had drawn the carts. They ran in little crowds, kicking their heels and lowering their heads; their gait was that of rocking horses, or small boats on high waves. All along the sides of the street, boys and men shouted and made little darts at them, grabbing at their horns. Behind the bulls came two riders in green-and-red stocking caps, herding them along, their horses tacking back and forth on the cobbled street, passing and repassing each other, rounding up the little bulls.

Still the young men on the sidelines teased the bulls.

"Oh, stop them!" said Francie, grabbing Mark's arm. "Can't somebody stop those boys?"

"My dear child, nobody would stop them. That's the whole idea of the running. The young bloods of the town want to show how brave they are," he said.

Just as he spoke, a boy more daring than the others ran straight across the path of a bull, in his eagerness to reach another on the far side. He tripped and rolled on the ground, under the oncoming animal's hoofs. Everyone shouted. The bull paused and lowered his head to sniff, but as one of the mounted men yelled and rode his horse straight at him, the bull ran away down the street. The boy rolled nimbly out of the way and jumped up, laughing, to join his companions in a doorway.

"Idiot," muttered Mark. "Now he'll have something to boast about all year."

It was over in a minute, a minute toward which the whole day had been aimed. The bulls turned a roped-off corner of the street and were gone from sight. They would be taken to the barns of the bull ring for the night. A sense of anticlimax pervaded the square. The young men sauntered away, or disappeared into the houses, and mothers with their babies and their excited older children climbed down from the benches. Soon nothing would be left of the *corrida* but the rugs hanging from the windows.

"Anyone hurt badly?" called Phyllis to Derek, who was chatting with a policeman.

"One man, a chap who lives near the ranch. He was badly hurt and this fellow thinks he'll die," said Derek. "On the whole, he says, it's been an unexciting day. On a really good day, it seems, they manage to kill two or three innocent bystanders."

"Extraordinary people," said Mark, sighing. "Well, if we want to get back before dark, we'd better make tracks."

"And tomorrow," thought Francie, "I'll really get started on my career as a great artist."

From the beginning Francie was interested in Catarina de Abreu. As the days went by and she grew to know the students better, the interest increased. Catarina seemed all that was romantic and tragic, with her large sorrowful green eyes and her clear, almost transparent skin. She was talented. Fontoura praised her work. She was married, Francie learned, and had two children, and her husband didn't approve of the art school.

A few of the students went every day for lunch to a small restaurant near Fontoura's. Francie was usually one of this group. She found she picked up Portuguese far more readily in this way than she did with the language teacher who came to Estoril now and then, in desultory fashion, to instruct Aunt

Lolly. Besides, it all seemed an important part of the school work; they were earnest young people who talked at length about painting and sculpture and literature. Most of the discussion was above Francie's head, she felt, not only because of the language. The talk was about things she didn't know. Therefore, during the stroll to the restaurant, or sitting at table, whenever some impassioned student galloped off on a monologue of the intellectual sort, she got into the way of chatting about personal matters with Catarina de Abreu. They tended to be de Abreu matters rather than Nelson, most of the time.

Catarina was forthright, imparting the most confidential facts with a lack of reserve which charmed Francie. Even an American woman, she felt, would not have told as much about herself as Catarina did, with the flat announcement, "I lead an unhappy life." And the details—the description of her husband's cruel mama, and his cold lack of understanding, and the general stresses and strains of being an artist in a materialistic world! It wasn't restrained, but it was decidedly interesting.

"Like reading an exciting novel," said Francie enthusiastically to Maria one afternoon. They were eating ice cream in their favorite tea shop, an enormous place of mirrors and dainty furnishings. Among the crowded tables you saw few men, but for long hours every day the ladies of Lisbon consumed cakes with whipped cream and drank tea in this shop, especially during the rainy season when it was not pleasant to be out of doors. Ruy hated the place, but when Maria and Francie were alone they usually went there.

"Catarina's almost too good to be true, isn't she?" continued Francie. "And so beautiful!"

"Catarina beautiful?" Maria looked genuinely surprised. "She is well enough, but I wouldn't have said she was out of the ordinary. Lisbon is full of women who look like Catarina. Perhaps we have different standards of beauty, you and I."

"We certainly must have, because I think she's stunning. Any of the men I know at home would fall all over themselves at the first look. And she's so young, too," said Francie. She sighed. "It seems queer that she should be married, and have two children, and quarrel with her husband and all that. She doesn't seem old enough to be a matron."

Maria said seriously, "Yes, it is a great pity that Catarina married so young. I think myself if they had left her alone and not persuaded her to marry until later there would have been less trouble now. With a little freedom beforehand she'd have made a better wife. But old-fashioned families, you know, don't look at things in that way."

"You seem to know all about her."

"Of course," said Maria. "We all know about each

other. Catarina's husband's family, the de Abreus, are connections of my mother's. I've known them all my life. I am really sorry for Catarina. I've always been, though she is so silly."

"Silly?" repeated Francie, displeased and a little shocked. "But she's very talented, Maria."

"Oh yes, she is *talented*." Maria said no more about the glamorous Catarina. Francie resolved to probe Ruy on the matter, and find out his opinion of Catarina's beauty, among other things.

When she had the opportunity to ask him he gave her little satisfaction. He merely shrugged his shoulders and said, rather as Maria had done, "Lisbon is full of women as pretty as Catarina."

"You only say that because she's a kind of cousin of yours," said Francie. "At home she'd be famous, I can tell you. People would be painting her portrait and everything."

"Then it's as well that Catarina isn't likely to go to America," said Ruy. "She is conceited enough as it is."

"I must say you're all awfully mean about her. She's not a bit conceited. You just don't understand her," said Francie. "Mark says she's a smasher."

"Ah well, of course that changes everything," said Ruy. "Though I don't know this wonderful Mark, I am now convinced."

"It's all very well to laugh, but you don't appreciate her enough around here," said Francie.

"I am not really laughing. I do not laugh when people are loyal and generous," said Ruy, "and you are both."

Such a compliment from an unexpected source threw Francie badly off balance. She simply gaped at Ruy, and he looked back with eyes full of kindness and admiration. "You are a very nice girl," he said.

"I thought you—well, I thought you didn't think so," she said idiotically.

"I do think so," said Ruy sternly. He decided to change the subject. "When did Mark meet Catarina?" he demanded.

She bristled at his tone. It sounded suspicious. The pleasantness of a moment ago was forgotten, and she said sharply, "He hasn't met her. Yesterday when he came to the studio to call for me he peeked in the door, that's all. He noticed her. Who wouldn't?"

"So you went out alone with this Mark after your class," said Ruy, without expression in his voice.

"Yes, I did. So what?" flared Francie. "Why not? It's the way we do behave in the States and England."

Ruy did not reply, and Francie felt ashamed of herself. She wasn't absolutely in the right, she knew. Aunt Lolly would remind her that the customs of the country must be observed. "I'm sorry," she said. "Isn't it done here? I thought—"

"It is quite all right for moderns," he said in gentle tones. "I was wrong to speak of it. Only here, you understand, our young ladies when they have no chaperones are careful to go in groups."

"Like you and Maria and me. I see," said Francie.

The conversation worried her when she thought it over later. Not that she was genuinely concerned about Ruy's opinion of her own behavior; she could trust him to be reasonable on a question like that. He had been to America and knew for himself. It was his attitude toward Catarina which seemed more unpleasant. She felt a sudden longing for Glenn and all the other Americans she had left on the other side of the Atlantic. *They* would have understood her. *They* would agree with her about such matters. It was appalling that so many nice people should have mistaken ideas.

"Women like me should stay at home, they say," Catarina had told her during one of her long heart-to-heart confidences. "They tell me I have no business to be painting. They think I do it only to get out of the house, to meet friends who are not of the family. They have such bad thoughts, you cannot imagine!"

Thinking of her plaintive little voice, Francie's indignation mounted. It was really disgraceful the way young people were managed by old people in this country. Look at Ruy himself, allowing his life to be ruined by a stubborn, silly father. He should have been a painter, she was convinced. Look at Catarina, being stifled and ill-treated. "Somebody ought to *do* something about it," stormed Francie to Aunt Lolly.

"Possibly," said Aunt Lolly, "but I'd be careful if I were you, my dear. It's not your affair."

Francie was silent. She had remembered one of Mark's sayings at Phyllis' dinner, "One doesn't want to go about reforming the world."

But one did want to—she was certain of that!

CHAPTER 7

WITHIN a few weeks, Francie's routine was so changed that she would not have known herself, even if she had had the time to think things over. Gone were the late mornings in bed, and the sulky, wistful hours of gazing out to sea. Gone were the empty spaces of late afternoon, when she idled, waiting for the telephone to ring. Portuguese evenings are long for an idler; she had dreaded nights when she had no party or gathering. But all that sort of thing was over.

"I go to bed early—that is, as early as I can, with the Portuguese late, late dinner hour," she wrote contentedly to Pop. "Otherwise I would oversleep in the morning and miss the train that gets me in for life class."

Francie was in truth an early riser now. With

difficulty she had persuaded the chambermaid to bring her chocolate promptly, and she always dressed quickly and left the hotel without disturbing Mrs. Barclay. It was all very much like schooldays in Jefferson, and none the less pleasant on that account. Sometimes she half expected to meet Ruth as she hurried from the hotel and across the road. The elm-shaded streets of Jefferson and the crisp Middle Western mornings, scented with burning autumn leaves, seemed to haunt the Lisbon streets, though the avenues were already languorous and heavy-aired with warmth when the train let her off near the studio.

Fontoura's classes themselves had that same half-familiar atmosphere, though her fellows were not at all like the young Americans Francie had grown up with. They were a different group, quieter yet more alive than her old friends. In fact, they were so unfamiliar to her that it was hard to decide why she was always being reminded of home in the studio.

"Just because it's routine, I suppose," she decided. It was more than the routine, however. Francie had become possessed with ambition, a feeling she had not had since schooldays. She was ashamed now of her slowness in beginning; she blushed when she remembered how she had sacrificed the first day of Fontoura's instruction. None of the others would have done a thing like that so light-heartedly.

And there was another thing: all these new friends

of hers, or at least nearly all of them, worked awfully hard. They weren't stuffy in any sense of the word, but they acted like people who were confident they would be artists, who wanted to be artists, and went about achieving what they wanted with a fervent earnestness that made Francie marvel.

"I don't see how they stick at it," she said once when Ruy asked about her impressions. "I mean, of course I know what it's like; I get steamed up myself about something I'm painting, once in a while. But that only happens when I'm sure I've got a good start. These kids are always steamed up; they *always* seem to feel they've got a good start. And they know how to make the start, every time. They're—" she paused, searching for an unusual word, but she couldn't find it. "They're keen as bird dogs," she said at last, for want of something better.

Ruy nodded. "Naturally," he said.

"But it's extraordinary," went on Francie. "What is it about Portugal that makes everybody like that?"

"Oh, but it isn't Portugal!" said Ruy. "You are in an unusual school, do not forget that. Every one of those students is hand-picked by Fontoura. He would not accept them for pupils at the beginning if he didn't find some special quality, some talent or industry—both, if possible."

"My goodness," said Francie. "You make me feel awfully inferior."

At this point it would have been nice, she thought, if only Ruy would reassure her, and say that she was just as good as any of Fontoura's favorites. But he didn't; his mind was still on the others. He said, "The little lame fellow, you know him? His name is Monteiro, I think."

"Yes, I know Monteiro, of course," said Francie.

"That boy comes of a very poor family," said Ruy, "a family of a poverty you cannot imagine. They are fishermen, and Monteiro too would have been a fisherman, like his father and brothers, but he wasn't strong enough, and so he took to drawing scenes of the sea. Fontoura found him on one of his sketching journeys on the coast. He has given him a scholarship out of his own pocket."

Francie was thoughtful. This information explained a good deal about Monteiro, she realized. During the lunch period, when she and her friends went out to the café, Monteiro never came with them, but went on with his work as if food meant nothing, as if there were not enough minutes in the day. He was always there in the morning before her, no matter how early she came. Come to think of it, sometimes she had seen him cleaning up the studio after class. "I suppose he works for Fontoura any way he can," she reflected. "I suppose he doesn't get a lot to eat. No wonder he looks quiet and thin."

The thought was disturbing.

"He is good, very good," said Ruy, "but he is not the only talented student there. Fontoura brings out the best in all those children."

Francie did not reply. She had learned to share the intense respect, verging on awe, that was felt by her companions at the school for their head master. She wished intensely that he would give her more attention. Twice or so in a week he paused by her sketchboard and gave a criticism. It was short, much shorter than the talks he gave some of the others, but after all she was a new arrival.

"And I guess he doesn't enjoy talking English too much, either," she told herself. Nevertheless she longed for the day when the master would treat her as he did the others. It wasn't only pride that made her want to fit into the class and get a word of praise now and then. It was a sense of duty; she felt she owed it to Ruy to make good. After all, she was there on his special recommendation. Besides, it would be nice to live up to Ruy's ideas of her. She liked his admiration.

"Could I possibly be falling for that boy?" she thought. "That would be awkward." Then she thought of Dom Rodrigo, and shook her head. He would be a terrifying father-in-law.

There was no one in Estoril or Lisbon with whom she could talk it over, and Francie was not a secretive girl; she liked talking about these things. All her life she and Ruth and the other girls in their select circle had tended to take their hearts out and examine them, and discuss them, and take note of any changes of sentiment. No yearning was too trivial, none too serious for these semi-public confessions. Now, during her morning train rides in this distant country she thought wistfully of the long, cozy talks she and Ruth used to have: Was Glenn a better dancer than Chuck? Whom was Ruth going to date for the country club dance? Wasn't Connie awfully young to be wearing Jimmy's pin?

"Kid stuff," thought Francie, sighing. "I'm grown up now, but I wouldn't mind wasting time like that again. It would help me get sorted out. And it was comfortable and easy-going. Sometimes the worshipful atmosphere at Fontoura's gets kind of rare for me."

To change her thoughts, which were growing gloomy, she pulled out her little sketch pad and amused herself with making up a new border pattern for a bedcover. It was just doodling, of course, but it was fun.

The students were in full strength that day. As Francie had noticed, there was little voluntary absenteeism among Fontoura's pupils, but the all-powerful call of family life had been known to intrude. Even with all the fervor in the world, a Portuguese painter might have to excuse himself from class in case of a funeral, a wedding or sickness of a close relative. There was one other exception sometimes—Catarina de Abreu. It was generally understood, if Catarina did not turn up, that she had been frustrated again by the ogres of her family.

Today when Francie came in and went to her locker, she was glad to see, as she glanced over to the Life section under the glass roof, that Catarina had already arrived. For nearly a week Catarina had been absent, and though the other students had not discussed it very much, the way they shrugged and shook their heads over her name spoke volumes. Evidently Catarina's husband, or mother-in-law, or second cousin once removed, had made one of the periodic de Abreu rows about Catarina's shameless behavior. A good woman did not neglect her children, they said. A good woman did not continue, in spite of all that her elders and betters could say, to go out in this stubborn way and spend the day without them, doing God knows what in some rackety *atelier* among bohemians.

Every so often it was all too much for Catarina, and then she gave in for a little and stayed at home. Francie had spoken of it indignantly to Mrs. Barclay.

"Isn't it a disgrace, Aunt Lolly? Isn't it a shame?"

"Yes," said Aunt Lolly, "it's a shame, I suppose. But she's wise to give in a little, if she doesn't want an open break with her husband's family."

Francie wondered if things weren't even worse than Catarina hinted. That husband! Francie had never seen him. He didn't come to Fontoura's; according to report he refused to set foot in the studio, or even in the street that led to it. "He must be a rat," Francie decided. "It wouldn't surprise me if he hit her sometimes."

Even if Catarina hadn't actually been a good painter, Francie thought, it was disgraceful that she should have to struggle so fantastically to do something innocent like attending an art class. And it was all the worse, since she *was* a good painter. Unfortunately, as Maria once said (rather oddly, Francie thought), she was very good.

"It would have been more convenient if that talent had been given to somebody whose life was not full of other interests," said Maria. "A woman like Catarina—" She left the observation unfinished, and Francie did not insist that she go on. It seemed wiser not to talk about Catarina very much with the da Souzas; on that subject they were always irritating, both of them. They lacked the slightest sympathy, thought Francie, for their downtrodden kinswoman. Perhaps it was only to be expected that they would take the national point of view, but it was disturbing, and disappointing as well.

Francie put on her smock, sniffing the air, as usual, with appreciation for the workmanlike smell of paint and wet clay. She carried her easel over near the dais and set it up.

"Oh, it's you, Francesca," said Catarina. "I am so happy to be back, you cannot think." She gestured as if words failed to express her happiness. "It is as if I had been years in a desert," she said.

Catarina never asked questions about the affairs of others. She didn't ask after Fontoura now, though he would have been the first thought of any other student after an absence like hers. This was typical of Catarina. All her talk, and she talked rather a lot, was about her own life and emotions. But somehow Francie did not find this trait as irritating in Catarina as it would have been in someone else. Catarina was so beautiful and tragic that when you talked to her it seemed quite natural and right that she should be the only thing that mattered.

"Really I have suffered," she now continued, pinning a sheet of thick paper on her stand with deft fingers. "Only my work, *my work*, would be worth all this suffering."

She looked pathetic and fragile. "Poor Catarina," said Francie. "It must have been very bad this time." She would have liked to ask questions, but she and Catarina would not be alone much longer. In the little anteroom that served as Fontoura's private office, she heard Monteiro moving about selecting supplies for the day.

Catarina said her trials had been inexpressible. "My mother-in-law," she added. "She was so cruel, Francesca. You would not believe her cruelty. For three days I have been in bed with a crisis of nerves, and even now, look at my hand, how it trembles. That is the worst. I am not able to work properly when my nerves are so tortured."

"Oh dear, Catarina, I'm so sorry. I am, really. I do wish I could help you," said Francie. "Anyway, you're here among your friends now."

Catarina sighed and began to draw. The door opened to admit three more students, and she only had time to say rapidly before they came over, "Francesca, never marry a Portuguese."

It sounded sinister. Considering her recent thoughts about Ruy, it gave Francie quite a shock. Had Catarina meant anything in particular? Francie stole a look at the other girl's grave profile, and decided she had not. She couldn't possibly look so innocent if she had been hinting.

There was a dinner party scheduled that evening for Mrs. Barclay and Francie, at one of the Lisbon hotels. Their host was an elderly British wine importer who had spent most of his life in Oporto. Mark was invited as a matter of course, because his father was Mr. Sinclair's friend. As for Mrs. Barclay, she had brought a letter to the Englishman from someone in

Paris. The two ladies hired a taxi, because Aunt Lolly did not yet feel well enough to brave the train.

Francie was unusually silent during the ride, and Mrs. Barclay looked at her inquiringly. She said, "Tired, dear? I'm afraid this going back and forth twice in a day is tedious for you."

"Oh, I'm not tired. Not in the ordinary way," said Francie, "but it does seem an awful waste of time, this social life." Aunt Lolly looked amused, and Francie went on defensively, "I suppose it sounds funny coming from me, but it's the way I feel. One party after another—what does it prove?"

"One art class after another doesn't prove much more, if it comes to that," said Aunt Lolly. "Too much of any one thing isn't good."

"You can't compare them," said Francie.

"Perhaps not, but it's a mistake, I think, to go in for any one activity exclusively," said Mrs. Barclay. "Of course I wouldn't like to see you satisfied with a completely idle life, but I wonder if you aren't inclined to be over-enthusiastic just now about this painting."

There seemed to be no reply necessary, which was fortunate. Francie couldn't trust herself to speak mildly. "This painting" indeed! She wondered what the reaction would be with the crowd at Fontoura's if she should repeat Aunt Lolly's speech to them.

Sheer amazement, most likely. They wouldn't understand Mrs. Barclay at all.

Everyone seemed determined to rub her the wrong way that night. Mr. Sinclair hit on another unfortunate phrase when he was talking about Portuguese life. He had asked Aunt Lolly if she'd met any of the local families.

"A few," she said, "those who are friendly with our American and English acquaintances, and they've been very kind. I must say I like the Portuguese way of life. I like their devotion to their families."

Mr. Sinclair was pleased. "That's very true. Yes, it's charming," he said.

"Devotion?" cried Francie in emphatic tones. "*I* think they're perfectly *disgusting*."

Everyone turned to look at her in surprise. "That sounds very convinced in such a young lady," said Mr. Sinclair mildly. "In what way are they so disgusting?"

"Oh, it's all hypocrisy," said Francie, thinking of Catarina. "The men pretend they're nice quiet types when really they're the most terrible tyrants. They're awfully mean to their wives."

"I say," said Mark, protesting. "That's a pretty sweeping statement. Anybody would think you speak from personal experience."

Mr. Sinclair laughed as if Mark had made a joke, and began talking to Mrs. Barclay about some less controversial subject. Mark regarded Francie with a puzzled, displeased stare.

"If you don't mind a word of advice," he said, "I'd go easy on the criticism if I were you. They're inclined to be sensitive in this country. Of course, I don't know just what called forth your outburst, but that's my advice for what it's worth."

"I'm entitled to my opinions," said Francie.

"Never said you weren't. Shall we dance?"

They danced. Mark seemed to have forgotten Francie's bad manners, but she was uneasily aware of a certain coldness that remained in his treatment of her. Francie didn't like undercurrents. She said impulsively, "Mark, I was wrong. I'm sorry I snapped at you. I don't know why I'm so crabby. I guess it's something I heard today at Fontoura's. I'm sorry."

He thawed immediately. "That's quite all right, poppet. I was sorry for poor old Sinclair, that's all. You gave him a turn, I think, speaking up like that. In his world, little school chits know their place." Francie laughed. "And speaking of Fontoura's," went on Mark, "am I ever to see something of this wonderful place, or is the door closed to outsiders? I've only had my nose in the door, remember."

"Well," said Francie dubiously, "I don't know. I don't suppose there's any reason you shouldn't come. They'd let you *in*, of course . . ."

"But you don't urge me, is that it?"

She hesitated again. "I'm not good enough yet," she said at last. "If you don't mind, I'd rather you didn't come for a while. Hardly anybody does drop in except other students, and people in Fontoura's crowd. People who *understand.*"

"I see," said Mark.

"When I think I'm getting along better," said Francie, "I would like you to come, honestly."

"Don't give it another thought," said Mark coolly.

"Oh dear," she said to herself, "now I've offended him again."

Uncomfortably she braced herself for a few words of rebuke from Aunt Lolly as soon as they were alone together in the car. Mrs. Barclay could hardly be expected to overlook her speaking out of turn as she had done at dinner. But to her relief, nothing was said until they separated for the night.

"Good night, my dear," said Aunt Lolly. "I wish you could sleep late tomorrow; I'm sure you need a rest. You did seem tired tonight."

"I'll be getting a rest soon enough. I forgot to tell you," said Francie, "that Fontoura's going away to an exhibition in Madrid, and while he's gone the studio closes down for a week or two. I'll have a rest whether I like it or not."

"Splendid!" said Mrs. Barclay. Nothing more was said about the dinner party.

CHAPTER 8

"I SUPPOSE it was a sensible thing to
come away on our own." Mrs. Barclay sounded as if
she didn't believe what she was saying; she glanced suspiciously around the unfamiliar dining room. "Obviously we are early for lunch. Now if we'd come on
a properly conducted tour—" She broke off and
looked reproachfully at Francie. They had come
rather suddenly on this trip, by ordinary bus, and she
hated impromptu decisions.

Francie laughed at her. "Be a big girl, Aunt Lolly,
and try to enjoy your adventure. You wouldn't be so
timid in France."

"People speak a reasonable language in France.
You know where you are with them."

"I know where we are now," said Francie. "We're
in Evora, enjoying every minute of it."

She went on talking until the soup came, gently teasing her godmother as gaily as she could manage, but her heart was not in it. Her thoughts kept straying back to the letter she was carrying in her handbag, right there on her lap under the table. It had come yesterday, and she had not yet spoken of it to Aunt Lolly, though usually she reported on every letter of Pop's. She had a feeling he didn't want her to mention it, even to Mrs. Barclay.

It wasn't at all the kind of letter she would have expected from Pop, because it was vague and he was always very downright. "Keep this under your hat," he wrote, "until I have a better idea of where we stand, but I just wanted to tell you we ought to cut down a little on expenses. I can't say any more as yet, but don't go in for anything that costs very much, not at the moment anyway. Wait till I give you the go-ahead signal, but don't worry."

Don't worry! How could she help worrying? Never in her whole life had Pop told her to be careful about money. There must be something very wrong if he was saying it now. Francie thought with a qualm of conscience about a number of her recent extravagances. That shopping trip last week, for example—and the fees for Fontoura! She had insisted on paying them all in advance, though it hadn't been necessary.

"I wish I could be sure it's all right to tell Aunt

Lolly," she reflected, "but Pop didn't say definitely that I might. I'll have to wait."

Mrs. Barclay was looking with alarm at the glass of wine that stood by her plate. "I'm sure we haven't ordered this," she said.

Francie said, "It comes automatically with the meal, I think."

Resolutely she put Pop out of her mind for the moment. After all, what was the use of worrying until she knew more about it? She sat back and looked at the surroundings. The thick walls of the Alentajano were faced with white plaster, on which hung gay, hand-woven blankets and a few medieval weapons. A barred window looked out on a court-yard and a whitewashed house gleaming in the sun, against the high, dark tower of the church across the square.

Francie said, "It's like being in a fairy story. I love the way their castles stick up on mountain tops, with roads circling round and round, going up. It's like the picture books I used to read when I was little."

"All Europe must have looked like this at one time," said Aunt Lolly.

After lunch they lost themselves trying to find their room. The hotel was an immense building, full of puzzling corridors and passages that took sudden twists, or went up or down by means of unexpected steps. It was a very old palace, and had been used as a combined prison and court of justice during the Inquisition. Thinking of this, Francie felt that the lower rooms would always be cold, no matter how brilliant and warm the sun might be out of doors.

"It's probably imagination, but it does feel much colder the minute you come in," she reflected. "Yet it was terribly hot in the bus. All those funny little cork trees on the way looked hot, too." She resolved to make a sketch of the cork trees now, before the effect was dulled in her mind. In the room, she began unstrapping her sketch-block.

"What are you going to do?" demanded Mrs. Barclay. "You're not going to paint here and now, are you?"

"I thought I might."

"But my dear Francie, we'll waste the whole afternoon if you do that sort of thing. Don't you want to come out and look at Evora? The book says it's the most interesting town for architecture in the entire country. Or at least, one of the most interesting."

"I might as well be on a conducted tour," said Francie in resignation. "Oh, all right. What a bully you are, Aunt Lolly!" She put down her sketch-block and with feigned resentment meekly trotted out of doors in Mrs. Barclay's wake.

They were soon lost, on the wrong side of the square. Evora is closely built, and carefully planned to save space on its steep slopes, so that it is almost impossible to see plainly where you are going unless you stand very high up in one of the towers. Resignedly the Americans retraced their steps and started off again in the opposite direction. This meant following a curving street like a cool white canyon between high houses, which went under an arch and suddenly brought them into a market square with a fountain, farther away than ever from their destination.

"Never mind, Aunt Lolly," said Francie. "We'll find your Temple of Diana if it's the last thing we do."

"But one feels such an idiot. Why, it was right there. I could almost have touched it through the window!"

Francie said, "I should have brought my sketchblock. I'd like to do this square. Don't let me go out without it again—that is, if we ever get back."

Fortunately they now happened on a shop that sold postcards and books and maps of the city, and there they got their bearings and started to work their way carefully back towards the Alentejano. " 'The Temple of Diana, so-called,' " read Aunt Lolly aloud as they climbed a steep cobbled road, " 'stands next to the Cathedral.' There, I knew it. Francie, where are you going? That isn't the way back."

"No, but let's save the Temple and follow one of

these bigger streets to the edge of town, shall we? We can't possibly lose our way now."

For an hour they walked outside the little city, near the great thick walls. Two men driving small donkeys loaded with firewood and vegetables passed them and said something in greeting; a little boy accompanied them quite a long way, chattering incomprehensibly; they met a family of girls and old women in black, who smiled at them. Everything was intensely quiet otherwise. The ground looked nearly as barren as the deserts of Arizona. For the first time since they had arrived in Portugal, Francie felt as if she were really far away from home, alone in a strange land. It was a good sensation.

When they turned their steps towards the Alentejano again, Aunt Lolly insisted upon stopping here and there to look at cathedrals. "We didn't come only to relax, remember," she admonished Francie. "We can always go for walks and picnics, anywhere in the world. This is a unique chance. My hip? It never felt better; this dry air is doing me a lot of good."

"I really think, Aunt Lolly, that this is the right way to go traveling. I'd rather go with you any time than anybody else in Portugal," said Francie. "It *is* a lovely place. We'll have to bring Pop and make a longer stay. But this is the right season, not too hot. I'm so glad Fontoura decided on a holiday just now."

Mrs. Barclay made absent rejoinder; she was trying

to negotiate cobbles and read the guidebook at one and the same time.

But it was Francie who spotted the building, which, though it had no sign they could read, nevertheless bore the indefinable look of a place open to the public.

"It's a kind of cathedral, I'm sure," she said. Mrs. Barclay hesitated, but an old priest or monk, who had been lurking within the darkness, settled it by making his appearance in the sunlight and motioning them to come in. Though Mrs. Barclay explained to him in her best French that they spoke little Portuguese he continued to talk as he ushered them through an anteroom where a few large books and holy figures stood about as if in a museum. They went down into a cellar, and paused at a door over which hung what appeared to be a fairly lengthy poem. Their guide waved his hand at the words, inviting them to read.

> *Nos, ossos, que aqui estamos,*
> *Pelos vossos esperamos.*

"I can't make out a word," said Francie in despair. "Does it make any sense to you, Aunt Lolly?"

"No more than to you, my dear. Isn't it miserable to be so stupid?"

However, they smiled gratefully at the old man and pretended for politeness' sake to have appreciated the legend. He led them through the door. Then he stepped back, smiling proudly, so that they could get the full effect.

They gasped. "What in the world?" said Francie.

"It's like the Sicilian catacombs, in a way," said Mrs. Barclay, "but I don't think they are anything like as elaborate."

They stood in a large room that seemed to be made completely of human bones. Hundreds and thousands of these grisly relics were embedded in walls and ceiling. Here the bones were chosen and arranged for their length, like giant matchsticks; there a number of differing lengths were disposed in the form of a star. One place was tastefully made of nothing but skulls.

"Is it real?" asked Francie in hushed tones. "Are they all genuine?"

Mrs. Barclay said that they were quite genuine. "I don't know where they all might have come from," she added, "but you can be sure there was nothing criminal in it. Probably somebody stumbled on genuine catacombs, or perhaps they were excavating to build a big palace, and came upon a forgotten cemetery . . ." She paused at the sight of Francie's face, which in the dim light of the cellar was rather green. "It's not meant to be horrible, you know," she said.

They had turned to go, and were in the middle of polite thanks to the old man when he suddenly lost interest in them. Other visitors were coming into the Bone Chapel. He hurried out to greet them.

"Who in the world, besides us, would be nutty enough to come here?" asked Francie.

The other party came through the door—three females in black. Francie looked at them carelessly at first, and then more fixedly. The youngest of the three women stared back. She moved closer, peering through the gloom.

"Francesca!" she cried.

"Catarina!" cried Francie. "What *are* you doing here?"

"I am with my cousins who have a *quinta* not far off. But you, Francesca, what brings you?"

Francie introduced her friend to Mrs. Barclay, but Catarina hesitated noticeably before performing her own introductions. She seemed reluctant, and Francie thought she detected a shade of fear in her eyes.

Still, the Portuguese ladies were amiable and courteous, and they seemed to take it very much as a natural thing that Catarina had made friends at art school. Francie understood enough of the language to know that Catarina was explaining her.

"I don't want to hold up your party," she said, when everybody fell silent. "Mrs. Barclay and I were just going back to the hotel. We stopped to see this." She gestured around her. "Catarina, do tell me if you can what it's all about. Is it really a chapel?"

"Oh yes. I always like to see it when I visit Evora."

"But whatever's the idea? It seems such a queer thing to have built. Do they hold services here or anything?"

"It is not that kind of chapel," said Catarina. "The people who built it thought the Portuguese might forget their spiritual duties. That little poem at the door—"

"Yes, do tell us what it means," said Aunt Lolly.

Catarina solemnly said, "It means, 'We bones who are here wait for yours.'"

There was a depressed hush, and then everybody said good-by.

Out in the air, Francie exhaled loudly and gratefully. "That awful place," she said. "Just think of running into Catarina there! I'm sure it means something."

Aunt Lolly said crisply that it merely meant Catarina and her cousins had been moved by the same spirit of sightseeing which activated themselves. "I see no reason for deeper significance," she said. They walked for a long time in silence.

"Oh, I'm sure there's more to it than meets the eye. Poor Catarina. She looks haunted, I think, as if something tragic is always there in her life," said Francie at last.

Mrs. Barclay sniffed. Then she said in gratified tones, "Here it is!"

Quite accidentally they had come out of a narrow street straight onto the Temple of Diana. It stood alone, exquisitely simple with its stone pillars and platform.

"That's something a lot better than any old bone chapel," said Francie. "Let's take a good long look at it. I want to think about it last thing tonight, and forget all those skulls."

Yet it was the skulls she remembered, as background to Catarina's delicately hollowed cheekbones and anxious, pleading eyes, until the thought of Pop's letter recurred to her and all other matters faded out. Francie did not sleep well that night.

CHAPTER 9

FONTOURA was back and his students greeted him with a glad burst of effort, all except Francie. The world, her own little troubled world, followed her into the studio where it had no business to be, and she could not rid herself of it. Frivolous thoughts of parties, speculations as to Catarina, and, most especially, unhappy wonderings about Pop came between the painter and her work so persistently that Fontoura evidently saw her lack of interest. He practically gave up giving her any criticism at all.

A week of this uneasy state of mind nearly drove Francie to confide in Aunt Lolly, though Pop had not given her permission to do so. At last, however, a second letter from him put an end to suspense. It was as he had hinted before: his business was in trouble. In the first letter he had ever written to his daughter about adult affairs, he explained it.

"Things are pretty tight just now, tighter than I can remember them being in years. Naturally we expected a slight depression after the war and the boom and I was prepared for that, I thought. But what with this upset in the Middle East and one thing and another—"

Francie read it through, struggling with unfamiliar ideas. She knew she ought to be worried; she suspected Pop would actually have wanted her to show a certain amount of dismay. But at first her chief feeling was pride that he had talked to her as an equal. Then she began to muse about Pop as a person.

She dropped the letter to her lap and sat quietly, thinking back; she had never before tried to sum him up in just this way. It was almost impossible to think of her father as somebody needing anything—advice, or companionship, or help. He had always been in the picture just to supply all this.

Francie thought of the genial daddy of her baby years, a large, reassuring creature who dropped in at Aunt Norah's sometimes, like Santa Claus, with his pockets full of surprises. As she grew older, of course he seemed to shrink a little, but he was still Pop, the ultimate mainstay, the person who loved her and tried to spend as much time as he could with her. This had not been a great deal. Aunt Norah had always explained how his work kept him away, moving around the world, working mysterious miracles for her sake. Francie had accepted the pleasant fact that she was the chief reason for the magnificent man's efforts; she had long since stopped feeling surprise or gratification that this should be so.

Oh, there had been moments when she felt grateful. It was sweet of him, she recalled, when he made that tremendous effort to be there in Jefferson the first time she went to school—all the way from New York he had come, for the great day.

"You're going to be a big girl, aren't you?" he had said. "You're a brave girl. You won't cry. If you don't cry, as soon as you come home we'll go downtown together and buy the best pencil box we can find."

"And if only he'd known," reflected Francie, "I didn't need all that agonizing. I was dying to go to school like all the other kids in the block. Still, I was awfully glad to have the pencil box, and the doll, and the dress . . ." Her eyes were wet now, but she went on remembering.

There was that day she starred in the dancing-school show. Pop was terribly proud of her. He couldn't be there because he was in Iran, but he cabled and ordered a grown-up bouquet, and it was carried up the auditorium aisle and presented to her at the footlights.

Then the year in England when she had been tiresome, and Pop was patient and understanding— He could understand when he had time, and when he didn't have time he gave her presents.

"I don't know anybody who used to get more presents," said Francie to herself. "I wish I could give him something now. Oh, I wish I could."

A thought struck her suddenly. Wouldn't it be much better all around if she went straight home and told him she wanted to help? She thought longingly of Aunt Norah's house in Jefferson, and the safety there would be there. They could forget all this adventure; Pop could stay at home and they could live quietly . . .

But Pop might not *want* to live quietly. Quietness in Jefferson sounded very nice, but when Francie thought of Pop, she couldn't see him living in retirement, even in order to be the hero of a pretty story about a self-sacrificing daughter. And there was the cost of her passage home. Perhaps he just didn't have the money for that. Not to mention the high fees she had already paid with such a grand gesture to Fontoura. Pop would want her to get the good of that money, now it was paid.

With a deep pang, she pictured Jefferson in a cozy little glow of homesickness. It would be lovely to go home now, and walk down Main Street with Ruth, looking idly into the store windows before stopping in at the drug store for a double malted. It would be bliss to go out with the gang on Saturday night to the Homburg Hat for a few dances. It would be marvelous to dance with Glenn again, and try to trick him into saying something polite for a change. Dear old Glenn, always criticizing her, but crazy about her just the same. A girl needed a boy like that, Francie decided sagely. A girl wanted a boy around whom she was used to, who was used to her. Oh, it would be wonderful to go home now to Jefferson, but—

"I've got to stay for the rest of the year," Francie told herself. "I've just got to."

She stood up briskly and went to the dressing table to fix her face, the reflection of which gave her a shock. She looked a woebegone being with her eyes red and her nose pink. "Oh, come on," she said to the girl in the looking glass, "you have it pretty good, after all. The girls at home would all give anything for your chances. A year abroad! What have you got to howl about?"

In that light, it all seemed much less gloomy. Just the same she wished she could help Pop. She sat down to write and tell him so.

The Japanese say, "Bees sting a crying face." Francie had written and stamped her letter before she remembered she had another envelope from America which she had not yet opened. Turning it over now, she saw the name and address of Peggy Pierce, one of the girls from Jefferson School.

"That goon!" muttered Francie, in unkind surprise, for Peggy was not at all an intimate friend. The others were rather afraid of her; she was quick-witted and malicious. "I wonder why she's writing to me? To tell me something I won't like, I bet."

Still, any word from home was welcome. Ruth and Glenn had both been dilatory lately, and Francie was cheerful as she slit the envelope. For two pages, Peggy was harmless. She prattled in a routine way about school activities, football games and so on. Francie was about to sigh with relief as she neared the signature, but relief departed suddenly at the last paragraph.

"What do you think of Gretta *now*? Personally I've always considered her a drip, and I never could figure out what Glenn sees in her, after you. I decided a long time ago it was a case of any port in a storm, and you're always somewhere on the other side of the map, so why not Gretta? But I could be wrong, and I'll tell you why we all think so. The other night at the Homburg Hat, when we were in powdering our noses, she opened her sweater a little while she was washing the old face, and I spotted a ring on a chain round her neck. Diamonds, no less. Not very big ones, but definitely diamonds. She saw me eying it and buttoned up but swiftly. Well, what do *you* think?"

"This is not a tragedy at all," said Francie to herself. "I don't really care the least little bit. I'm not in love with Glenn. I haven't any right to hang on to him. I couldn't expect anybody to go on waiting while I rush off to Europe all the time . . ."

She crumpled up the sheet of paper and threw it on the floor, and put her head down on her arms to think it over.

"I am *not* crying," she told herself sharply. "Or if I am, it's because of Pop. I'm not homesick or unhappy. And I don't mind a bit if Glenn's engaged."

Outside the window the spring sky deepened to a brilliant blue, and narrow whitecaps curled along the edges of the waves. The early morning procession of fisherfolk was thinning out; the broad boulevard began to hum with motor cars. In a chapel near the beach, a bell rang, and Francie sat up, seized with swift alarm. Nine o'clock! She would be awfully late to class. Mechanically she made up her face. It badly needed it after so much emotion .

But what did make-up matter anyway? Nobody really cared the least bit whether she was attractive or not.

"Romance isn't the only thing in life," she thought. "I'll be a famous painter instead, and then they'll be sorry. Glenn will be sorry he didn't write to me, and Peggy will be sorry she did. *I'll* show them."

She rushed out, slamming the door. A chambermaid in the passage stared after her and shook her head, disapproving such American, unladylike haste.

CHAPTER 10

GOOD resolutions are fun to make, and for a time they are quite as satisfactory as genuine good behavior. Francie was not late to class for nearly a week after her determination to devote her life to Art, and she didn't leave class early, either. There came a day, however, when Mark tempted her.

"If only you weren't working at this ridiculous studio," he said tentatively, "we could get an early start tomorrow afternoon and join Phyllis and the others for a picnic. But of course you take your work so seriously!"

He looked past Francie as he spoke, into Aunt Lolly's eyes, and Francie realized that he and her godmother had arrived at some sort of understanding concerning her. They were drinking tea in the hotel lounge. Aunt Lolly gave Mark an encouraging nod, and he went on, "How about giving it a miss, just this once?"

Francie hesitated. "It's the others," she explained. "They never knock off, or at least hardly ever. Not as much as I do, anyway."

Mark looked around toward Mrs. Barclay, who said in a decided manner, "My dear, you mustn't overdo it. You're not settling into Fontoura's for life. This was supposed to be a combination year of work and pleasure for you. After all, I meant to give you a gay time in Paris. I've made enough of a muddle as it is with your plans, and if you turn into a little drudge, your father decidedly is not going to thank me."

"Oh, he wouldn't mind at all, Aunt Lolly, truly he wouldn't. It *is* time I got serious about something." Francie spoke earnestly. "It makes me ashamed when I look around at all the other students. You see, they behave like professionals, and they can't understand why I don't. And really, why shouldn't I, too?"

"Because you're not," said Aunt Lolly. "Because you haven't made up your mind yet. At least I hope you haven't. A girl your age ought to take a little time off for gaiety."

Gaiety? In her self-dedicated mood, this word shocked Francie. She looked dubious.

"Very well," said Mark. "If you won't come tomorrow, you won't, I suppose. I'll make other arrangements."

"I didn't say that," said Francie hastily. "I just meant I don't like the other students to look scornful at me when I walk out, the way they do. Still, this once won't hurt, I guess."

"Of course it won't," said Mrs. Barclay.

"You'll come, then," said Mark in satisfaction, and they discussed other things, and after a little while he left. Francie made a decision. Perhaps Aunt Lolly could help with advice.

"Aunt Lolly," she began, "I don't think Pop has written you, but there is something you ought to hear about." She told the story, and they talked it out—Pop's crisis, and her good resolutions, and the whole thing. Mrs. Barclay listened with calm attentiveness.

"I'm sorry now I didn't go straight to you," Francie ended, "but I wanted to figure things out for myself if I could, and act like a grown-up person for once. It's about time."

"Naturally you felt that way, Francie." Aunt Lolly spoke promptly, as she always did, as if she had a pattern that everything, no matter how unexpected, would fit against in one place or another. "It was your problem and you had to think it out. But now that you've allowed me in on it, may I give you just a bit of advice? Don't worry so about your father. It's not a catastrophe. It's merely a reverse, and he'll weather the storm. You'll see."

"But *he's* worried, Aunt Lolly."

"Of course he is, dear; he wouldn't have told you if he hadn't been. But worry is one thing and despair quite another," said Mrs. Barclay.

"Oh, *despair*." Francie dismissed the word. "I don't mean it that way. It's because Pop oughtn't to be bothered at all that I'm upset. He's used to being successful. It must be so horrid for him not to be."

Aunt Lolly smiled indulgently, and the smile irritated her god-daughter. While she talked with calm good sense, pointing out that Pop had not always been at the top of the tree, Francie was thinking in a new, detached way about her. Aunt Lolly was wonderful; everybody knew how wonderful she was. But did she always know best? For the first time, Francie entertained this startling idea.

Aunt Lolly *had* always known best, she now protested to herself. Aunt Lolly had been the refuge whenever Pop didn't understand. She had been a comfort when life with Aunt Norah in Jefferson seemed limited; she was an escape, and she never failed. Yet, she, the all-wise, was not understanding just at this moment. She was being as dull and placid as Aunt Norah could ever have been. She was standing between Francie and the once-despised, now longed-for Jefferson. One might almost have said that she was taking all the fun out of Pop's ruin. It was all very strange.

"I'm being awfully nasty," thought Francie with remorse.

Aloud she said, "All right, Aunt Lolly, I'll calm down if you think I've made too much of it."

"Depend on it, your father didn't want you to change your plans radically," said Mrs. Barclay. "You'll help him best at this time by going on almost exactly as you were, though naturally we'll be much more careful about your expenses. And do please relax a little about all this painting, Francie. I've said it before, I know, and I hate to harp, but relaxing is *so* important. This is your playtime, and you ought to have it no matter what happens. You can't help your father anyway."

Francie was silent. Why couldn't she help her father? It was nonsense. Aunt Lolly was talking nonsense, which was unbelievable.

"You have plenty of nice companions," Mrs. Barclay added. "*Wise* ones."

"You mean Mark? You mean I ought to see more of him?"

"That's entirely up to you, darling. I'm not trying to fence you in, or marry you off. I would hate to see you married to a foreigner and living so far away from America, but all that is your affair and Mark is a nice boy. So is Ruy. The world's full of nice boys!"

"You sound awfully frivolous, Aunt Lolly."

Mrs. Barclay sat there looking startled, as Francie made for the elevator.

In a stormy mood she went on the picnic with Mark next day, and in a stormy mood she returned. The others agreed it had been a successful party, but then it always was a successful party, Francie reflected. Nothing ever happened—nothing real or vital. Nobody did anything surprising; nobody's parents were in financial difficulties; the only excitement in all Portugal, for a foreign girl, was somebody snubbing somebody else at a party. It was not her idea of Life.

Back the day after, in the studio, she heaved a sigh of relief, for here at least she felt, or fancied she felt, something of what she really wanted. All the students were concentrating with intensity on their work, she mused as she looked around. Tomas, the man everyone said was sure to win a prize and a scholarship in Paris, had been there when she arrived a quarter of an hour early, too absorbed in his preparations to notice that she had come in. He was working with big gestures at a very small canvas. The Norwegian girl, the little old man, Catarina and all the others trickled in and set up their work to the tune of comfortable, desultory chatter before the model took her pose and silence fell.

How very strange that Aunt Lolly could not

understand this impulse that moved the students. "All this painting" indeed! Francie felt lofty as she thought of the Philistine attitude, compared with her own. Aunt Lolly meant well, of course, and so did Pop, but unless you are a real painter, a real artist, you can never understand.

"And it is no use trying to talk about it," she said to herself, absently watching Catarina at work. "It is no use trying to express in words what it feels like to be doing something on your own, really creating."

So rapt was she in this thought that she never realized until Fontoura came in that she herself had created nothing that morning. Then, naturally, it was too late. Fontoura walked over and looked at her painting which was just as it had been two days before, and for a little while he said nothing. Francie felt herself growing confused.

"I haven't got down to it this morning, somehow," she said at last.

"So I see. Thinking about yesterday's distraction, perhaps?" He passed on then to look at the Norwegian's work. Somebody behind her laughed a little. Francie did not like to whirl around and see who it was, though she longed to do so. But probably it was just a laugh about something else entirely, nothing to do with her at all.

Still, she didn't feel comfortable about having

taken that day off. It was no use trying to explain to people outside—she was repeating her thoughts, they seemed to run round and round in a circle, but it was no good at all explaining to Aunt Lolly. Pop might have understood a little better, if he wasn't distracted just now by his business difficulties.

At lunchtime, Francie felt unequal to facing the usual chatty student group at the meal in their customary haunt. She went over to Catarina and asked her in a low tone if they couldn't go somewhere else, just the two of them alone. Catarina was delighted, or at least said she was. "I like to be with you, Francesca," she said, "all the time. You are so sympathetic."

They went to a restaurant near the middle of town, and had a good long orgy of talk, all about Catarina's troubles. A detailed story of a dispute between Catarina and her mother-in-law carried them through most of the meal.

Francie said, "You know, you really shouldn't stand for it."

"But what is one to do, Francesca?"

"It's all *wrong*," said Francie. "It's your baby, isn't it? You're the mother and surely you ought to know what to feed it, and how to doctor it. Just because older women think they know best—"

Catarina said gloomily that it was not merely a matter of thinking. "She is so sure she knows best. That is it," she explained. "I tell you something, Francesca. I do not mind this one thing, this little thing. It was only today, and is worth no quarrel. My mother-in-law adores the child and means it for the best. But what is killing me *here*—" she slapped at her breast—"what is killing my soul is that they will not leave me alone. It is I, it is *myself* they are smothering. I am a wife, yes, I am a mother. But I am something more, and they do not want it."

"Oh dear, oh dear," said Francie.

Catarina took a bite of crème caramel, smolderingly. Her eyes glowed with pride and rage. Francie looked at her admiringly.

"These people do not understand artists, that is it," said Catarina at last.

"I know," said Francie.

CHAPTER 11

"THEY don't understand," said Francie to
Maria and Ruy. "Do they?" Maria's face was lit
up with intelligent sympathy. Ruy, always more in-
scrutable than his sister, nevertheless nodded deeply.
It was all calculated to make a girl feel much better
about—well, about what? What was it that worried
Francie so much, these beautiful Portuguese days?
For worried she certainly was, if not unhappy, about
her work, in a way she could not have expressed.

There was the matter of Pop, of course, but Francie did not feel frightened about herself or him; she
was only awfully sorry, and wanted to help. Pop had
become a romantic figure, like someone in a turned-
around legend; a man rather than a damsel in distress.
The idea hardly bore a closer look. Pop was a perfect
darling, a wonderful man and all the rest of it, but

his rotund self in business clothes bore no slightest resemblance to a young knight in durance vile. Nevertheless—

"Nobody understands about my father," continued Francie. "Naturally, I want to go and comfort him. He needs me."

"It seems like your duty," said Maria, but there was a certain amount of reserve in her voice. Portuguese girls did not so lightly strike out to do their duty, when they were assured their duty lay otherwise. And Francie had already informed the da Souzas that Aunt Lolly was firmly against any change of arrangement. Maria adored Mrs. Barclay; anything she said must be right.

"Besides which," continued Francie, "they expect me to carry on with the same old round. Parties, tennis, picnics, boating. Quite as if I were not really serious about things. As if Fontoura's were just a fill-in, sort of."

This time it was Ruy who reacted in a satisfactory manner. He simply lit up. "I know," he said. "It is what people always do."

"They never understand," said Francie again, and in a companionable silence they walked on, toward the entrance gate of the Feira Popular.

Maria had suggested a visit to this little Coney Island place, as something Francie had not yet seen of Portuguese life. Within a high brick wall, among booths where native handwork and little dolls were sold, where you could try your luck at shooting or having your picture made, there flourished small patio restaurants, coffee parlors, and amusement gadgets like scenic railways. Everything was lit to within an inch of its life; the Fair visitors wandered in a happy pool of yellow electricity, red neon, and flashes of the railway headlights when the little train swooped about overhead.

The three friends strolled around idly, paying little attention to the ordinary exhibits. Ruy knew exactly what he wanted to look at. Every so often the Government put on a special show of something particularly Portuguese. It was not supposed to be like the permanent exhibition in the Museum, where life-sized figures displayed peasant costume, and entire carriages were set up; the little Feira gallery was more likely to contain some modern sculptor's work, or a collection of antique dolls, especially lent for the occasion.

"Here it is," he said at last, gratification in his voice, "and you will be interested, Francesca. I hoped this was what they were showing this season."

Francie was delighted, for the little room was given over entirely to textiles of various sorts, from rare brocades to brilliantly printed coarse cotton. It was the kind of thing that always caught her eye.

"Oh, do wait just a minute, Maria," she begged. "I've just got to take notes on some of these."

The da Souzas paused and amiably watched as she dug a small sketch-block and pencil from her handbag, and began to copy down one of the patterns. They were used to her enthusiasm. All Portugal is accustomed to eager people drawing or painting, in the most unlikely places, and Francie had long since lost any self-consciousness she might have possessed about sketching wherever she felt the urge.

For a while the da Souza party had the room to themselves. Ruy, growing bored, strolled to the door and then outside, where he kicked his heels and watched the crowd of visitors. A couple of young men brushed past him on their way in; their clothes and general appearance attracted his eye for a moment, because he was puzzled. Were they English or American? One could not be sure; one only knew that they were not Latin.

Indoors, the blond man leaned over to take a second look at an embroidered shirt on display under glass. He said to the dark man, "Ravishing."

The English word, and the intonation, made Maria, like her brother, prick up her ears. Like him she was puzzled to say which the speaker was, English or American? She resolved to ask Francesca. But Francesca was too much wrapped up in her work to have heard at all, so Maria remained silent.

The two men moved with a sort of delicate assurance around the room, glancing carelessly at some things and with careful attention at others. Then the dark one spoke, and his voice settled matters for the interested Maria. He was certainly American.

"Pretty routine on the whole," he said.

"Routine?" The fair man sounded disapproving. "You're spoiled, that's the trouble with you. A week ago you'd have gone crazy about it."

The dark man shrugged. "We've seen so much of it. But it's still good for a page, I suppose," he said discontentedly. His tour had brought him close to Francie, and now he noticed her for the first time. As his shadow fell across the sketch-block, she moved and glared at him, disturbed. Ignoring her glance, he drew up to her shoulder and took a long, leisurely look at her work.

"Oh, I say," he called over his shoulder at his companion, "this isn't bad! Come and look."

Francie, hushed by astonishment, merely stood there meekly, while both men examined her drawing and looked at the print from which she had taken it, evidently comparing them.

"Interesting," said the blond man at last, in the tone of one making a concession. "She's done a really interesting modification there. I wonder if she's a professional? Have they professionals here, do you think?"

"Oh, I don't think she's a professional," said the dark man disparagingly. "I wouldn't quite call her a professional."

They inspected Francie as if she were a wax figure. Maria had gasped, but Francie was too staggered to do even that.

"You might ask," said the dark man at last. "Try her in French, Jim."

Francie found her tongue at last. "Please don't try me in French," she said. "I couldn't bear it."

The pause that followed seemed endless. Then the dark man laughed and broke the spell. "Let that be a lesson to you," he said severely to his companion. "How many times do I have to tell you that nobody ever turns out to be a native?" He said to Francie and Maria, "I'm terribly sorry. Really I am. One tends to assume that everyone in Portugal is Portuguese; the thing is we're so used to Spain where people honestly and truly *are* Spanish—"

"And can't speak a word of English," added the other man eagerly. "We get into careless habits, that's the truth of the matter. I suppose you're all dyed-in-the-wool Americans. Anyway, we are. My name's Jimmy Bryan, and this is Will Adams, and we're making what might be called an ill-will tour of the Southern countries. Now what about you?"

He smiled disarmingly at Francie.

"You're wrong again, or two-thirds wrong," she

said. "My friends Miss and Mr. da Souza aren't dyed-in-the-wool, or anything like it. But I'm sure they will forgive you."

Ruy had drifted back into the room, and was listening in surprise. Now he and Maria hastened to agree as politely as possible. Francie observed that they looked a little stunned, as well they might, by the rapidity with which the acquaintance was developing, but she was sure she could make it all right as soon as she had a chance to explain more about free-and-easy ways among Americans abroad. For herself, she was excited and thrilled, because she had recognized Adams' name. He was a designer whose word was becoming law—a new law—in the fashion world, a man who traveled around seeking out, among other things, new textile weaves and patterns for the upholsterers and dressmakers of America and England. He and Bryan asked eager questions about Portugal, about which they seemed to assume Francie was an expert, an attitude which embarrassed but flattered her. They had just arrived, they explained; they were without cut-and-dried plans as to how they were to proceed with their exploratory work. Bryan was the technical man of the party, who took photographs and checked up on materials, manufacture and so on, whereas Adams had the original inspirations.

"We're supposed to be spending our time in Spain, actually," explained Adams. "This is just a side trip.

No doubt you've heard about the great thing in Spain? Oh, everybody's there, simply everybody; people are going to Spain now for their clothes and Paris is tearing its hair."

"That is surely an exaggeration?" asked Maria timidly.

Jimmy laughed. "Of course it is. Will always exaggerates," he said, "but the fact is, Spain *is* by way of becoming a center of the trade just now, and so we've been there, in residence, for some months. This trip was a sudden notion. I suppose you've come out from the States direct?" he asked Francie.

No, she said, as a matter of fact, she wasn't in what he called "the trade" at all.

"But you will be," said Adams confidently. He gestured toward the sketch-block. "You're bound to be. You *look* the part, too. It's obvious."

Francie was not so sure if she liked that or not. She was not a mere textile designer, she told herself; she was a painter, an artist. However, it was nice to be treated with respect by such a famous man.

The five of them repaired to a little coffee house nearby and spent a pleasant hour with Ruy and Maria giving the Americans advice and suggestions. When they all parted, it was in a blaze of good will, address-swapping and making vague appointments for the future.

"That's what I like about America," said Maria during the ride back to Estoril, "the informality!" Looking wistful, she relapsed into her own thoughts, coming out only to say, "We had better not speak of the manner of our meeting to Papa, Ruy. That is, if these young men do call on us, as they said they would."

"Naturally not," said Ruy in lofty tones.

Francie listened in amusement only slightly tinged by impatience. How hemmed in everyone was in Portugal! "I may lose my patience sometimes with Aunt Lolly," she reflected, "but at least I can always tell her everything like this, and she laughs when things are funny." It made her more contented with her lot—for the moment.

Those two men had really been impressed by her interpretation of the design at the Feira Popular. It was not what she wanted to make her name at, of course, but any appreciation was pleasant. "Let's face it," she thought, "I need it, after the cold-shoulder treatment I've been getting from Fontoura at the studio lately."

"That is the way I like to see you," said Ruy, suddenly breaking into her thoughts.

"Why? How?"

"You look happy," said Ruy. "Stirred up and happy."

"Smiling like a kitten," added Maria.

Francie smiled more broadly.

"Aunt Lolly, I was thinking—" Francie began impulsively, and then stopped short.

"Yes, dear?"

"Never mind. For a minute I forgot the new Economy Drive, and it was a silly idea anyway."

Mrs. Barclay looked over the edge of the Paris *Herald Tribune* thoughtfully. "It might not be so silly. Tell me."

"Well," said Francie, "it was an old-fashioned thought at best. I was just going over in my mind the people I owe a little attention to, and it seemed to me some kind of party might have cleared up the whole picture. You know, Mark, who's been taking me around, especially to the Club. And Daphne and all the crowd. And I'd like to do something about Art School and the da Souzas, of course, and those American designers I told you about might like the chance to meet some people."

"All at one party?" asked Mrs. Barclay in slight surprise. "But my dear, they'll never mix."

"They won't have a chance, since I'm not giving it, but I've often thought we may be making a mistake anyway, Aunt Lolly, keeping worlds separate the way we do in your circles," said Francie earnestly. She leaned forward to emphasize her point. "If everyone always says, 'Oh, they won't mix,' and never does anything to make them mix, why, of course they don't mix! See?"

[141]

Mrs. Barclay smiled. "I see that you believe it," she said, "and that's enough for an experiment. Shall we do it?"

The excitement died out of Francie's face. "But of course we can't," she said. "With things the way they are for Pop, I can't afford it."

"I think you can," said Mrs. Barclay, "if you're careful. Why not ask Phyllis if you can't use her house? I'm sure she'll be quite willing, and then you won't be running up a bill here. As for refreshments—"

"Oh, Aunt Lolly, if only I can use Phyllis' house! And refreshments are only coffee or punch or something and little cakes. Of course I can do it. Of course I can. You're a genius."

She ran to the telephone.

CHAPTER 12

FOR a time it looked as if Mrs. Barclay's misgivings would turn out to be justified. Francie discovered it was not at all easy to plan one of the mixed parties she approved of. It seemed that she might offend people. To be sure, the British were not touchy; instead, they were amused. Phyllis said she thought it would be "a riot," and Mark puffed at his pipe and grinned as he thought of the possible repercussions.

"It won't hurt to stir them up a bit," he admitted.

But the Portuguese, especially Maria da Souza, were taken aback when Francie blithely talked of her plans. Said Maria, "Well, it may be all right, Francesca, but my mother, for instance, will not like the idea of meeting so many people she does not already know. I am sure she will not like it."

"But why?" asked Francie. "She needn't see them again, after all. I'm being awfully careful to do it formally, with invitations way ahead and everything. She can come, and go, and forget all about it if she's so displeased with the way it turns out."

"It is bound to be necessary to see some of them again, perhaps. You don't *live* in Lisbon, you don't know the difficulties." Maria looked worried. "I myself want very much to come to your party, you see. If Maman sends her regrets, then I am sure she will keep me home as well."

Francie hesitated. It was Ruy who spoke up and settled the question. "She will come, Maria," he said. "I will make a special effort to persuade her, and as for Papa, it does not arise; he will be in Oporto."

"Oh, if Papa is away—" Maria's face cleared. Obviously Papa had been the real trouble.

"Do you think I dare invite Fontoura, Ruy?" Francie spoke hesitantly. The idea had been buzzing in her mind for several days, but she had been too shy to ask. "I really do want to invite everybody at the studio," she added, "and as it's his studio, it seems so rude not to include him. Or do you think it would be presumptuous?"

"My dear Francesca, he's not so important as all that!" Ruy laughed. "Only a few of us think him very great, you know. He has no pride, no swelled head, and there is no reason he should have."

"Then you think he might come?"

Ruy said, "I could not say. He's not very social, especially when he's working hard. But he might enjoy it. He might possibly come and it can do no harm to invite him, at least."

Ruy was throwing himself into the preparations with genuine gusto, Francie was amused to observe.

"I'm interested for a special reason," she confessed. "I'm going to ask those two American designers we met at the Feira, and I wanted them to see Fontoura. They'd be so glad to meet him."

Ruy's face changed expression. He looked impassive, and Francie knew he was displeased. "But really," she said to herself, "I can't always be looking out for Ruy's complexes. He's either jealous, or thinking I have been forward. Or both. I can't help it."

Without compunction, then, she telephoned Adams and Bryan, and got Jimmy on the phone. "It's angelic of you," he said promptly. "Of course we'll come. As a matter of fact, Chère Mystérieuse—do you like that name? I made it up this minute—I intended to suggest that we pay a call on you this afternoon when we come out to Estoril for a swim. Will you be home, you and your aunt?"

They did drop in, glamorous and attention-getting in their brilliant sports shirts. They seemed to like Mrs. Barclay, and she was completely captivated by them, though Francie, who was inclined to be more critical, thought their manners rather casual for a Portuguese hotel. Will sauntered about as if he owned not only the building but the world it stood in. He put on spectacles when he came across a picture that interested him, then disdained the picture and stood on the veranda overlooking the sea, as if he were thinking of remodeling the Estoril landscape.

Jimmy caught Francie's anxious glance. "Pay no heed to Will," he advised her. "He's always that way—one foot in sea and one on shore. It's really that he's thinking of his work. We came over to see you for a reason, you know. Will had an idea."

"Oh? What was that?"

Jimmy lit a cigarette before replying. "It's that design you were drawing the other day," he said. "We liked it."

"Oh. Thank you ever so much, but it wasn't mine, you know. I just took it off that thing in the showcase," said Francie.

"No," said Jimmy, shaking his head. "You didn't. You *derived* it, dear. There is a difference between deriving and merely lifting. And your adaptation was clever."

Francie blinked at him. She could feel Mrs. Barclay's surprised admiration. A delicious glow of self-esteem crept along her veins. "Well . . . thanks," she said.

Jimmy said, "Have you got the drawing handy, by any chance?"

"It's up in my room. I'll get it."

She rushed over to the elevator, and was soon back on the veranda with the sketch-block. Bryan took it and studied it carefully, blowing smoke at it.

"Yes," he said at last, handing it back. "It's still good. I thought I wasn't wrong. Do you know anything about preparing a design for textile reproduction, Francie?"

"Not a thing," said Francie. Wonderingly she exchanged glances with Aunt Lolly, who remained quite quiet in her corner at the table, waiting to see what was happening.

Jimmy called Will Adams over and waved toward the sketch-block. "I got it out," he said, "and she'll do it up for us if we show her how. Won't you, Francie?"

"Why," said Francie, "if I can. I mean, I just don't know—"

"We're buying it, natch," said Will. "Do you know the rates?"

Francie said, in desperation, "Listen, boys, I don't know a thing about this. I don't know what you're talking about, even. Rates for what?"

"Designing," said Jimmy. "Look, if you will work this out for us in the convention we need—it doesn't take very much training—we'll buy it from you outright, for—well, let's see, will a hundred dollars be all right? To encourage her," he added in explanation to Mrs. Barclay. "It's the regular professional rate."

"Why, I'm sure that's delightful," said Mrs. Barclay. "What do you say, Francie?"

"It's *marvelous*," said Francie. "It's perfectly marvelous. But are you absolutely sure you want the design?"

The men laughed. "Perhaps not absolutely," said Will, "but that's our offer this afternoon, and if I were you, I'd grab it before we change our minds. Now then, if you'd like to learn something about the way to work them up, we'll show you. Where is your pencil?"

When they had gone away, a wildly excited Francie was hard at work, measuring out units on big sheets of paper.

"It is certainly very nice," said Aunt Lolly. "But what a surprise!"

"Mmmm," said Francie, bending over her work. " 'Nice' is a funny sort of word for a miracle."

The delirium of discovering herself to be a genuine world's worker was enough to send a more experienced girl than Francie off the deep end. When she woke up the next morning, it was hard to remember that merely twenty-four hours before she had found all her life's interest in a mere party list.

"Well, perhaps it wasn't my *entire* interest," she told herself in tardy self-defense. "Art comes first, of course, no matter what happens."

Nevertheless she lay in bed longer than she should have done, dreaming of the future. The designers had implied that this need not be a mere flash in the pan. If she found more amusing patterns, they would buy them. In time, thought Francie, she would be able to save up some money. She could support herself and tell Pop she wouldn't need more checks. She might even be able to help Pop with money. How surprised he would be! How proud of her! And how proud she would be of herself! Francie's imagination leaped ahead with the grace and ease of a mountain goat. She was holding court, in her mind's eye, at Pop's New York office; the staff was thanking her in their honest, inarticulate way for having saved their jobs along with the oil company. Francie was just about to make a little speech, modestly disclaiming any particular merit, when the chatter of the hotel housemaids outside her door reminded her with a horrid shock that she should have been up quite a long time before.

She jumped out of bed and dressed in a tremendous hurry, for a while. But even then she lapsed into a dream between shoes, sitting there on the bed with a sandal dangling from her hand. She was nearly an hour late at the studio.

Fontoura was already there when she came in. "Just like him," she thought resentfully, "making an early round the one day I'm so late!" As he had already been on her side of the class, she hardly expected him to return and look at her work. However, he did. When he had examined everyone else's, he came over and looked at hers, and when she thought about it later she felt it would have been far better for her spirits if he had not done so. He was severely critical.

Fontoura was always a hard taskmaster; he was well known for it among the students. Actually, however, he usually spared Francie. His comments when he made them to her were short and restrained, to such an extent that Francie often thought uneasily he was making a special case of her for some mysterious reason. Today she had no cause to complain of this. Fontoura was in a mood, and he worked out some of it on her.

As always, his English left a good deal to be desired, but he said enough for her to get the general idea. Francie lacked sweep, he said; she was tight and finicky; she must learn to let go. She must try to see things in the large. Something held back her imagination and her hand. "Relax," said Fontoura. "You are supposed to be painting, not making a pretty little design for a teacup or a handkerchief."

He always spoke loud and clear when he made his

observations, and the students of the class would not have been human if they hadn't listened in to everything he said. Francie, though humbly nodding, was terribly embarrassed. In fact, she was angry. Had anyone told him about her triumph yesterday with the Americans? But that was impossible; she had not told anyone herself. Nobody knew, except Aunt Lolly—not even the da Souzas.

Then she rebuked herself for exaggerating. Fontoura often talked this way when he was wound up. It didn't mean anything special. She wouldn't let it get her down.

That noon when the class was eating lunch, Tomas mentioned Fontoura's attitude toward Francie's work. "He was harsh," he admitted, "but you must not mind. He never spares anyone."

"It is for their own good," said one of the other boys quickly.

Tomas replied, "Perhaps it is, but sometimes Fontoura is much too overbearing. A style is a personal matter. Good as he is, who would want us all to be so many duplications of Fontoura? He holds us with too tight a rein. It is the fault only of a very good artist, but it is a fault. Now, when he spoke to me last week about my color . . ."

Some of the students burst out in excited protest of this speech against their idol, while others were on Tomas' side. The conversation turned into its accustomed path, and the discussion continued as it always does in any art class in the world. Francie's criticism was forgotten, save by Francie herself, but the more she thought about it the angrier she became. After all, why should one not design teacups and handkerchiefs? Could the world go on forever without teacups and handkerchiefs? Of course it could not and she suddenly said so aloud.

The other students paused in their squabbling and looked at her in surprise. This claim was a new one in their circle, and they needed time to think it out.

"But Francesca," said Catarina at last, "it may be true, what you say, only I do not think it should apply to us, here at Fontoura's. We are all here because we love pure art. Isn't that true, Tomas?"

"Certainly," said Tomas.

"I don't doubt that for a minute," said Francie, "but I just don't see why we shouldn't have pretty cups and scarves as well, or why it's a disgrace to be able to make them. Now, as it happens, I have become a designer myself."

After that it was Francie's hour. In the fascinated silence, she told her friends all about the amazing thing that had happened to her. She began to appreciate it herself even more in the telling. Had she not become a professional?

"One hundred dollars!" repeated Catarina after the climax.

"One hundred dollars," said Francie affirmatively.

Everyone was silent again. Then Tomas said, "It must be tempting. Yes, it must be very tempting."

Francie looked at him sharply, for his tone seemed to lack enthusiasm.

"When you think of what Monteiro lives on," said another student, a girl. "That poor boy . . ."

"But he could never design for the Americans, I am sure," said Tomas. "Monteiro is, in the end, an *artist*."

It annoyed Francie terribly, but what could she say? It was unreasonable to be annoyed, and to feel as she did that her triumph was tarnished by the students' reception of it. She resolved to be more sensible. To prove to herself that she wasn't disappointed, she said, "I'm working on another design already. I should think if I try, I might sell them quite a few in a year. Don't you think so, Catarina?"

Catarina agreed; everyone agreed. They all beamed at Francie's good fortune. The little spurt of ill temper, or jealousy, or whatever it was, disappeared, and they were all cheerful when they returned to their painting.

"There, that showed them," Francie reflected. "I bet even Fontoura will respect me more when he hears I'm a wage earner."

She recovered herself from another attack of dreaming, just in time to do a little more work before the end of the afternoon, but it seemed rather tedious to be slogging away at figure work like this when she could be so excitingly employed at the drawing board at home. Once she caught sight of Catarina staring at her. The Portuguese girl's look of admiration and envy was startling. Catarina looked like a prisoner watching a bird high up in the sky.

"I'm an awfully lucky girl really," thought Francie, and felt ashamed of all her recent discontents.

Besides, Mark was waiting at the hotel when she got home, to take her out to tennis, and now that she had broken the news at Fontoura's she felt free to boast a little to him. His reaction was most gratifying.

"Good stuff," he said heartily. "You really should come up north, you know. Guimarães, up beyond Oporto, has shops and shops with printed stuff in all sorts of Portuguese color arrangements. You'd have a picnic there. You *are* an amazing woman, aren't you? Prop of your father's old age, I shouldn't be surprised. Why, we'll have you designing for us before we know it, settled down in our place in Manchester with a contract."

"Not for me," said Francie, "not if I know it. You won't find *me* messing around with floral patterns in pink and blue."

"No, but you might work on the prints we send

down to West Africa. They like their colors violent there," said Mark, "and I think your style would be just the ticket."

Francie swung at him playfully, and they went out to the car.

CHAPTER 13

THE party was taking place at last. All sorts of exciting things had happened to the guest list since it was first thought of. Francie had known all along that she could depend on the English contingent, but there were so many unknown factors apart from them that she had hesitated as to the amount of refreshments to order. However, it looked as if there would be a record attendance. Dona Gracia had said she would be there with Maria; most of the art class, including Catarina, had cheerfully accepted; even Fontoura was coming. He had taken it as a normal thing that he should be asked, just like any plain human, and Francie was exultant. For the first time in all these weeks she began to feel like a genuine member of the studio group.

[156]

The only sad thing about the prospect was that she would not be able, after all, to present her new friends the designers to the assembly. Jimmy and Will had suddenly and capriciously gone back to Spain— "Before they saw half the things they ought to see," Francie reported in sorrow to Mark. "I'm afraid I'll have to admit they aren't really serious about wanting to understand Portugal and see everything. It seems there's some kind of silly party in Barcelona they said they couldn't possibly miss. Jimmy suddenly remembered it. You know how capricious he is. And off they went by the very next plane. I can't understand people like that." She looked mournful.

Mark said Portugal no doubt hadn't been interesting enough for the boys. "After all, Lisbon's a tidy little place. I expect they aren't too fond of tidy places," he said.

"Whatever do you mean by that?"

Mark made a wide gesture. "Their type, you know —they probably prefer crowded bistros, and knifings by dark. Hollywood excitement and all that."

"But Portugal *is* like that, if you take the trouble to look," said Francie indignantly. "It's terribly romantic. All that wild country in the South, and the hills and so on in the North that you are always talking about. I think they've been very silly to go so soon."

"They can always come back," said Mark soothingly. "No doubt they'll return just as easily as they went away. Americans do move around easily."

Francie was not reassured. "I feel as if they'd snubbed the place," she said, "and besides, we do not move around as easily as all that, Mark. I've been here for months, for instance."

"Oh, you. You're different; you seem to be settling down here." He glanced at her obliquely. "How's Ruy?" he asked after too short a pause.

Francie ignored any meaning he may have hidden away in the question, and said Ruy was very well. "He's supposed to come in early to give us a hand," she added, "but I don't think it's necessary really; the servants at Phyllis' are marvelous. Well, shall we get going?" She took a last look in a mirror by the door. "Do I look all right?" she asked.

"You do indeed. You always look all right," said Mark.

"Yes," thought Francie, "it's all very well to say, but you never really look at my clothes. I wish most men would pay more attention." Now, the designers —but it was no use yearning after them. They had gone. Not irrevocably, however. Will had bought another pattern from her before they departed, and Francie had their Barcelona address in case she had any more good ideas. "I'm really launched," she thought happily.

Smaller preoccupations and anxieties now filled her mind as the party began. The guests arrived in a trickle at first, and then suddenly the house seemed crowded, and she and Mrs. Barclay were badly rushed, trying to keep track of everyone and see to it that people were introduced. Francie was able to notice with absent-minded amusement that Dona Gracia had found a familiar friend in the rackety crowd, and gone off to sit in the far room, away from everybody. Portuguese women always did congregate together, like Orientals, she reflected. The men, like the women, from sheer habit formed their own little cluster, defensively, as far away from their wives as possible. The only exceptions were the young students, who refused to be overawed by custom, and maintained a sort of coeducational group between these two extremes.

Francie, carrying plates around, tried to check up on her guest list. Fontoura was there, chatting to Ruy and another young man and looking very much at ease; she hoped Aunt Lolly would find some opportunity to talk to him before the end of the party. Tomas was there; Monteiro was, too, looking rather shy and hungry. Most of the girls from the studio seemed to have arrived as well. Only Catarina was still absent.

It did seem a pity, Francie thought again, that Jimmy and Will couldn't be there. But at least she had her new, second triumph about the designs to comfort her, and she went over to tell Maria about it. Maria's excited congratulations led Francie to tell more people; the word spread, until everyone from the studio had heard the story. Fontoura heard it from Tomas; he raised his eyebrows in polite surprise and looked at Francie as if he had never really seen her before.

Into this little scene of triumph came Catarina at last. She swept into the room like a prima donna: there was something wind-swept about her, wind-swept and tragic.

"Francesca!" she cried. "I have ruined your party, I am so late."

"Not at all," protested Francie. "I'm glad you made it." She glanced expectantly at the doorway, but Catarina had evidently come alone.

"My husband is desolate, but he could not come with me," said Catarina, interpreting the look. She added mysteriously, "I will tell you later," and turned away to greet one of the studio crowd.

Time passed. Francie realized suddenly that she was tired and hungry. In her zeal, like many another hostess, she had forgotten to sample her own refreshments. She slipped out to the kitchen and collected for herself a plate of ice cream and a glass of fruit juice which she brought back to the party. Then, hesitant, she looked around for somewhere to go. Her own and Mrs. Barclay's efforts had been all too successful. Everyone seemed happily occupied, and there was no place that she wanted to edge in on; she felt she would be intruding on all the groups.

"Besides," she thought, "I don't really want to make formal conversation just now."

Near the kitchen door she spotted a comfortable little corner, which on most mornings, she knew, was a breakfast nook for the family, screened off from the main room by a thick growth of indoor plants in flowerpots. This afternoon the maids had moved the breakfast-nook furniture except for a single chair and a small table which they had used for a serving place.

"Just what the doctor ordered," Francie said to herself. Unobtrusively she went over, sat down, and began to eat her ice cream.

For a few minutes everything was peaceful, if not quiet; the conversations that drifted near and far from behind the screen of vegetation didn't bother her at all. She was comfortable and resting. Besides, most of the talk was in Portuguese, and though by this time Francie could understand a good deal of Portuguese when she tried, she was still able to wall it off from her ears when she didn't want to bother.

Once, something Derek said as he came near her

vicinity made her prick up her ears. "You heard about Francie's great success?" he said to somebody. "Jolly good, isn't it?"

A girl's voice replied in amiable assent. Without recognizing it, Francie accepted the good will. She smiled to herself, took a big bite of cake, and sighed happily.

A moment later the whole success came crashing down.

Of all people, Aunt Lolly was involved. There was no mistaking her voice, even if Francie hadn't seen her looming near, over the plants. She came along with Fontoura, talking as slowly and carefully as he did. They picked their way among the English words with caution, and they were in the middle of the conversation when they arrived opposite Francie's chair in the corner.

"—is not admirable," he was protesting. "I did not say that. But you ask me what talent your daughter is showing, and I must be honest."

Daughter? Aunt Lolly had no daughter, Francie thought; she was stupid for a moment.

"Francie is my ward," Mrs. Barclay corrected him. "Do you mean, then, that the child is not an artist?"

"There are artists and artists," said Fontoura. "I set myself to train one kind, you understand—one kind only. My kind of artist is perhaps limited in numbers. I want the very best. I want nothing but the first-rate."

"Francie has always been very clever with her pencil," said Aunt Lolly in rather hurt tones.

Francie, rooted to her chair, was so much taken by surprise that the fundamental rules of behavior were completely forgotten. She knew perfectly well, in the ordinary way, that one should not eavesdrop, particularly when people are talking in private about oneself. But she simply forgot. This was a matter so tremendously important that she forgot what she was doing. She leaned forward to listen better. Fontoura and Mrs. Barclay had by this time found chairs and were settled down just out of sight, but well within earshot.

"She is clever," said Fontoura, and Francie imagined just how he said it, with an impatient little bow of the head. "She is very good for the second-rate, but she is not a genuine painter."

"But she is so much better than the average! I don't know anything about art, and I don't pretend to, Mr. Fontoura," said Aunt Lolly, "but I know what all her teachers in America said. And just look what has happened in the past few days. Those clever young men who bought her patterns—"

"I heard of that," said Fontoura. "I heard of that. I am very glad of it. I congratulate you and your ward. But it proves what I had always suspected—" Here he became so agitated that his English was hard to understand, even for Francie who was accustomed to it. The burden of his remarks, however, was that Francie would never be of the caliber he demanded of his pupils—that her very facility in designing was one of the things that held her back. Francie felt that he resented her having done this work for Will Adams; he felt somehow insulted that anyone from his choice studio should have descended to outright commercialism. Fontoura said he had always felt doubtful of Francie's promise. He had been persuaded, however, because of his friendship for Ruy, to accept her. He had then felt bound to the bargain by the fact that Francie paid for all the courses in advance. But now, talking it over with Mrs. Barclay thus, he said he was emboldened to suggest that he refund the money that was left over, and let Francie go at the next convenient stopping point in the course.

"It would break her heart," protested Aunt Lolly. "I wouldn't know how to tell her. It seems so unnecessarily cruel!" She was extremely distressed.

Well, yes, admitted Fontoura, it did seem savage, now he looked at it with her eyes. Of course such extremes were not necessary. The matter could wait.

"She can at least finish the year," said Mrs. Barclay, "and then she'll be going away from Portugal in any case, and she need never know. I must say, Mr. Fontoura, I think you place too much emphasis on this matter of the designing. You seem almost angry about it."

"I *am* almost angry," said Fontoura simply. "I see you cannot understand."

"No," said Aunt Lolly, "I can't. It's a different point of view."

There did not seem much else to say, and they soon moved away.

Afterward, Francie sat like a marble statue. Later she could not have said how long she was there. At first the shock made her numb. She actually felt as if she were suspended in mid-air, unable to breathe; there were no other feelings at all. Then as she began to feel ground under her feet, pain returned.

The first few minutes were very painful. It has happened to almost everyone before they reach Francie's age—that someone or something lets them down; they are disappointed and betrayed in something they believe, or one of their loyalties is outraged. It had happened to Francie too, but never with such a blow.

She wasn't an artist after all. Or Fontoura was wrong. Or he was jealous and spiteful, and to admit this to herself was almost as bad as to think she was a poor artist who had been making a fool of herself. Aunt Lolly, bless her heart, had done her best, but Francie knew that Aunt Lolly didn't understand the peculiar problems involved in this matter.

Anyway, it began to dawn on Francie as she sat

trembling in her corner that the biggest pain of all, at least for the moment, was not whether Fontoura had let her down, or whether she was the kind of painter she wanted to be. Neither of these questions mattered as much as the overwhelming fact that she was in the wrong in the one inexcusable way: she *had* made a fool of herself.

There was no other way to put it. She had forced herself into a class where she wasn't wanted, and remained there in spite of all the other pupils' ill will. (It seemed that way to poor Francie, shivering as if her skin had been taken off. It seemed that way for several hours.) She had swaggered about, boasting of her success with Adams. She had wasted Pop's money just at a time when it mattered most. She had been shamed in the eyes of Aunt Lolly. Goodness knew what the da Souzas must have been thinking of her all this time. All the people who had been kind to her—yes, probably the English too, even though Derek *had* sounded normally friendly when she overheard him—everyone in Portugal had really been wanting to laugh at her all the time, but they were too polite to show their feelings.

Francie stood up. She clenched her fists. She must not show anyone how agitated she was. This was her party, and she must not embarrass people. That was more important than anything. So she stepped outside, after a decent interval to allow Mrs. Barclay and

Fontoura to move well away. Neither of them saw her come out of the sheltered corner, and nobody noticed anything out of the way in her behavior.

It was time for the guests to be going. Evening parties go on for a long time in Portugal, but they come to an end at last, and some people had already made their excuses and departed before Francie saw Catarina approaching.

"May I wait a minute, Francesca, and talk to you alone?" asked Catarina in an urgent whisper.

Francie's heart, already overburdened as it was, sank lower at this. She was usually more than ready to listen to Catarina, but tonight she wanted only to get rid of everybody, even Aunt Lolly, and be by herself to examine her wounds. She still felt a little stupid and anesthetized; she knew there would be worse hours ahead, and she wanted to get them over with. She had to figure it all out: what a failure she was, how nobody loved her, how everyone was only putting on an act of being fond of her. Even Glenn had deserted her, hadn't he? Even Glenn . . .

But Catarina seemed really to need her company. Francie said, "Of course, dear. Why not drive back to the hotel with us as soon as all these people are gone?"

"I dare not," said Catarina. "My husband."

Francie stared at her, only half listening. She had been a fool, all these months in Portugal. She would never live it down.

"My husband," said Catarina in rapidly mounting hysteria. "He forbade me to come out tonight, and I defied him. So now he will perhaps make trouble for you too, Francesca. Please, if he does, forgive me. I must go."

Francie was listening now. She reached out and grabbed Catarina's arm. "Catarina," she said, "do you ever get *desperate*?"

"Of course. I am always desperate," said the Portuguese girl proudly.

"Desperate enough to—to *do* something about it?" asked Francie. She breathed fast.

Catarina looked at her wonderingly. They stood at the head of the veranda steps. At the end of the driveway, Catarina's car was waiting, and Mrs. Barclay had begun to glance toward them in a puzzled way.

"I want to get out of all this," said Francie. "Why not come with me? Good-by, Catarina. I'll talk to you tomorrow."

Catarina's eyes shone with excitement as she kissed her hostess good-by.

CHAPTER 14

MRS. Barclay must not be allowed to suspect anything about the eavesdropping. In the first painful hours, Francie held on to that idea instinctively, not because she felt guilty—she didn't—but because her head seethed with angry plans, from which she didn't want to be dissuaded. She wasn't angry with Aunt Lolly particularly, but Aunt Lolly was part of the whole infuriating landscape, and Francie wanted to forget about it all as soon as possible. To forget the world in which you are, it is necessary to find a new one. So Francie bided her time and made her plans.

In a less hectic atmosphere she might not have been able to conceal her agitation, but Phyllis' house was upside down, as it naturally would be after a party, and none of the people Francie had to deal with had their minds on each other or on her. They were obsessed with cleaning up and superintending the servants, and disposing of the extra china and napery that had been dug out for the occasion. Through all the hubbub of the last hour there, to add to the mix-up, Mrs. Barclay's health gave cause for belated concern. Phyllis' mother kept declaring Mrs. Barclay was more tired than she would admit—that she *looked* tired.

"You're quite sure you feel all right? Such a long evening for you, I'm afraid. I do wish you had spent more time in your chair," she said anxiously.

Mrs. Barclay replied, over and over, "I never felt better in my life, my dear. Don't fuss. The doctor said I ought to exercise the leg, you know. Sitting down all the time is the wrong thing. Really. *Really.*"

"Aunt Lolly," began Francie, "do please go on ahead to the hotel."

"Definitely not, my dear."

Such conversation carried through quite a lot of time, and when at last the American women did get back to the hotel, Francie was able to pack her Aunt Lolly straight off to bed, without any post-mortems. After that, in her room, she sat for a time at her desk with her pen in her hand. The situation seemed to call for a letter to somebody, a long exhaustive discussion of what had happened, how she felt, what steps she was considering and so on. But who would be a worthy recipient of such a letter? Two or three years earlier it would, of course, have been Ruth. Today, Ruth was out of the question. She had been out of touch with Francie too long; she wouldn't understand. Glenn? Oh no! Glenn was gone forever; he was engaged to that pudding-faced Gretta. Besides, Francie had an uneasy feeling that if Glenn knew what she was thinking of doing, Gretta or no Gretta, he would try to take a hand in it, and she didn't want that. He would be firm and officious. He might even appeal to Pop. "Pulling the heavy uncle act," mused Francie.

At this rate nothing was getting done. It was awfully late, even for Portugal where people often don't go to bed until well past midnight. Francie yawned and wondered for a sleepy moment what all the excitement was about, anyway. Habit was overwhelming her. Wouldn't it be simpler and pleasanter to pretend nothing had happened, to forget everything she had overheard Fontoura say, and go to bed, and trot off obediently to the studio in the morning?

No, it couldn't be done. Deliberately she remembered the conversation and went over the worst of it, word for word, until she was hot with anger all over again. Go back to the studio?

"I'd be fried in oil first," vowed Francie. She opened her purse and, for self-confidence's sake, took a good long look at the check the designers had sent her, then she ate an aspirin tablet and climbed into bed. Funny to think that she wouldn't be in this comfortable room, using this pretty bed, very much longer.

Even so, Francie got up and dressed and went off to the class in quite the routine manner, next morning. She had it all thought out. If Friday had been one of Fontoura's routine days for visiting the studio and criticizing, she would not have been able to face the prospect, but she knew he never came on Friday; he had commitments in another part of the city, helping out a friend at a private studio. Francie was not keen to go on working as if nothing had happened, but she had to keep in touch with Catarina, and unless the other girl rang her up, there was no way to maintain the contact. Never yet had Francie dared to brave the redoubtable de Abreu, his mother, or any other dragon of a relative who would, she was sure, always answer Catarina's telephone first in order to check up on the captive.

It was all thought out, but as Francie approached the familiar alleyway that led to the studio door she wondered, nevertheless, if she could see the program through. How many of the pupils realized what the master really thought of her work? Would he have been unkind enough to take one or two of her contemporaries into his confidence? This was quite possible, and more than possible. He was an impulsive man; discretion was not one of his qualities, as she realized all too well after yesterday's experience.

"No matter what he thinks about me," reflected Francie, "if he had any tact he wouldn't have talked that way to Aunt Lolly. After all she *is* my guardian here." It surprised her that she could think even this dispassionately about Fontoura. She had spent a large part of the night trying to find a cool place on her pillow, and hating him.

The studio looked perfectly normal. Two of the girls, thinking they had been inadequate in their thanks yesterday for the party, hurried over to Francie to make up for the gap. Quietly Francie accepted their compliments; quietly she brought out her painting materials and set to work. From the other side of the model's dais, Catarina gave her a watery smile. Silently a pact was formed. They would meet at the lunch hour and talk matters over—it was understood.

Francie started to paint. Her efforts were unsuccessful. At every stroke of the brush she seemed to feel Fontoura's eyes on her hand, and hear his voice rebuking her for not painting wide, sweeping streaks of color.

"What difference does it make anyway?" she asked herself in despair. The feeling swept over her suddenly, just as if she hadn't been trying to control herself all evening and night. It seemed to break on her all over again that she was not a great artist and never would be, in Fontoura's expert opinion. Now, for the first time, she felt not only anger and shame, but genuine grief. She had lost her pride, she had lost everything.

"How can I ever face the people at home? And Pop—oh, how can I face Pop, ever again? He believed in me so much!"

Francie's head drooped lower over her paints, and she held her breath to keep from sobbing aloud. She simply must not. Even if it weren't for the embarrassment involved, she would not be able to tell kindly, anxious inquirers what she was crying about. No, no, there must be no sobs and no tears. Francie swallowed, breathed hard, and sat up again, triumphantly dryeyed. No one had noticed anything.

"At last," said Catarina. She looked over her shoulder conspiratorially as the girls sat down in the little restaurant.

"Good heavens, Catarina, they didn't follow us," said Francie. "Nobody knew we were slipping away. I don't think anybody from the studio ever comes here."

Catarina shook her head wisely. "One never knows in Lisbon, Francesca; I am very much watched. I am never, never sure of not being followed."

"Oh, you mean—?"

"My husband," said Catarina, her eyes lowered. "He would not hesitate to use spies. Especially after last evening. You know, Francesca"—she hitched her chair forward and talked with breathless earnestness across the table—"last evening I was afraid for my life. Really *afraid*. There was such a look of rage in his eyes! Because I came to your party without his permission."

"Did he *beat* you?"

Catarina did not reply, and Francie's heart swelled until she could control herself no longer. "It is outrageous," she said. "It's horrible." She burst into tears. They were the morning's postponed tears, but Catarina couldn't have known that.

Catarina was overcome by this evidence of sympathy. Clearly she had not expected quite such enthusiasm in her friend. "You have a good heart, Francesca," she said at last, "but you must not feel so deeply. You make me sorry I have told you anything." Again she looked nervously over her shoulder, but this time it was in embarrassment rather than apprehension.

Francie wiped her eyes and spoke more calmly. "It wasn't because of you that I cried, Catarina; it's only that it all seemed too much, all of a sudden. You see I had rather a shock yesterday."

"Oh, I am so sorry. What was it? Bad news again from your father?"

Francie hesitated. "Would you think me very impolite if I don't tell you yet, Catarina? I can't bring myself to talk about it yet."

"Ah yes, I can understand that," said Catarina. "I understand that very well. You are *sensivel*—sensitive, that is—like me. We have much in common."

Gloomy as she was, Francie permitted herself a faint glow of pleasure in the thought that she might be considered akin in spirit to romantic Catarina. Then she addressed herself to the matter in hand. Briskly she began, "Catarina, I *will* tell you one thing. Never mind why, but I've decided I just can't stay on here any more, living in Estoril and going to the studio."

Catarina looked surprised and excited. "No? But Francesca! It must be, yes, I am sure it is a love affair, an unhappy one of course. No, do not tell me if you don't like. I understand. I understand everything. When the heart is involved—"

"It is not a love affair," said Francie. "It's something else. Something far worse."

"It is not that handsome Englishman?" asked Catarina, ignoring everything but her thoughts.

"No, no, no. It's not a love affair at all, Catarina."

"I do not think it could be Ruy da Souza," said Catarina, "so I think it must be the Englishman, and you do not wish to tell me, quite naturally. But you could trust your secret to me, Francesca. I would never—"

"I tell you it's *not* Mark, or any man at all," said Francie, beginning to feel impatient. "It's ever so much more important than just men. Catarina, do, please, listen and stop jumping to conclusions."

"Very well, Francesca. I am listening." Catarina folded her hands on the table like a good girl at school. "Only remember, if it is Ruy you are thinking of, a Portuguese husband is no good, and especially a Portuguese husband from *my* family. I know what I say. In Portugal, the husbands . . ."

"Catarina, once and for all, I don't want to talk about husbands, or romance, or men, or love, or anything like that. I am *serious*. I want a serious talk."

"But my dear, darling Francesca, that is just what I am trying to have! So. What are we to talk about?"

Francie lowered her voice. "I am going to run away," she said. She sat back to survey her effect. "What do you think of that?" she asked.

Catarina's brow wrinkled with the effort to understand. "Run away? But you said you do not wish to talk about men!" She looked reproachful.

Francie sighed. "I don't. I'm not planning to run away with a man. I am going alone—"

"Alone?"

"Or take you along with me," said Francie triumphantly. "There, that surprises you, doesn't it?"

The word "surprise" was an understatement. Catarina looked staggered. "Take me with you?" she repeated at last. "But where? And why? Do you return to your father in New York? I do not think—"

"No, no. New York is absolutely the last place in the world I want to go. I wouldn't have to run away, anyway, if I meant to go there. Nobody could stop my going back to Pop," said Francie, "but he's got troubles enough of his own right now, and I decided against it."

"And Mrs. Barclay, she approves of this idea?"

"Oh, goodness." Francie sighed a little. Catarina certainly didn't seem very quick on the uptake this afternoon. "Listen, Catarina. If Aunt Lolly knew I meant to run away, and approved of it, you couldn't call it running away, now could you? No, of course she wouldn't approve. That's one reason I'm not telling her. . . ." Francie's voice wavered as she remembered the other reason, but the angry thought of Fontoura spurred her on. She took fresh heart. "I want to get out of all this, and I think the best way is just to slip out quietly without telling anybody or saying good-by," she said.

"You are wonderful," said Catarina. "All Americans are wonderful. Such women as you are! So brave! So independent! You say, 'I do not like something here,' and immediately, without waiting, you are off. And all alone! Oh, you are wonderful, Francesca."

Francie was willing to believe it. She felt very hungry for appreciation, after what she had heard about herself the day before. She let Catarina go on in this vein for some time before cutting her off, but the lunch hour was drawing to a close, and she had no intention of returning to the studio that afternoon. It was necessary to come to a decision with Catarina.

"Are you really very happy?" she asked abruptly.

"Why, Francesca. You know my life. How could I be happy?" asked Catarina. "It is my fate to be miserable."

"Oh, that's just *silly*," said Francie violently. "Talking about Fate, I mean, and all that. Things are what you make them."

Catarina waited, her velvet eyes fixed on Francie's face. She realized there must be more coming, and Francie did not disappoint her.

"You ought not to accept it," Francie said severely. "It isn't right to live the way you do. It isn't natural."

Catarina made a bewildered gesture. "What else can I do?"

"It's hard to tell, now, unless you take my advice," said Francie. "You might have done something when you first married, like making your husband take you to some other house, for instance, where all his awful family couldn't pick on you. But you didn't, and now I guess it's too late to get anywhere like that."

"It was always impossible," said Catarina flatly. "You mean well, Francesca, but you don't know them; you cannot possibly say. In Portugal a bride does not tell her husband where they are to live." In spite of the prevailing mood, she laughed at the very idea.

"That may be so," said Francie. "I can't argue because, as you say, I don't know. But I do know one thing: you shouldn't go on the way you are, living with them. It's too awful. I don't know how you've stood it all this time. Listen, Catarina, I can't tell you much; I can't tell you why I'm going away. But I can say where I'm bound for, and if you want to come along, once you know, I'd be more than glad to have you. It's something to do with my new work. You know, my designing."

She spoke self-consciously, because it all seemed strange and impossible even now. Catarina, intuitive for once, nodded without speaking. Francie continued,

"Well, these men who gave me the jobs, the Americans, you know—they've gone on back to where they came from."

"To America?" asked Catarina.

"No, not America. They're staying in Spain for a while, I don't know how long. I don't suppose they do either. They always move on just when they want to."

"Spain?" Catarina was listening carefully. "Madrid, I suppose?"

"They're in Barcelona," said Francie, "and my

idea was to go and look them up there, and ask if I can't do some more work for them right on the spot."

"There!" said Catarina with a cry of triumph, "I knew it was a man. You said not, but I know. Which is it? The good-looking one with yellow hair, or the other?"

Francie sighed again, and thought for a disloyal moment that Catarina might with justice be called unduly obsessed with romantic notions. But, of course, it was merely the way she had been brought up, Francie reminded herself. She decided to be very patient and gentle. For a long time she reasoned with Catarina and parried all her friend's arch remarks and suggestions. No, she said over and over, her interest was not sentimental. No, not at all. No, she couldn't explain at the moment why she felt so angry and disappointed in Lisbon. Some day she might tell Catarina, but not yet.

"At any rate," she said, when she felt she might lose her temper if she stayed on the subject much longer, "I'm going to Barcelona. Whether or not you believe I'm chasing those men, I'm going to Barcelona. Now, what I want to know is, will you come with me? I'd love it if you would. I don't much mind about the rest of Lisbon; the way I feel right now I wouldn't care if I never saw any of the others again. But I'd be worrying a little bit about you, Catarina. It's—

it's all wrong that you should have to live the way you do, with your talent and everything. It's all being wasted because of your home life."

"Francesca," said Catarina, "you are very good." Her eyes were wet. She reached out and touched Francie's hand. "If I could come with you, I would, this minute," she said, "but I can't. My dear, I have no money. I never have any, not even for the tram. My husband sends me everywhere in his car, and he pays for everything. I cannot come with you to Spain."

"But I've got my design money," said Francie, "and that would get us there. Then when I begin to earn more money, regularly, we'll be all right, and you can really paint, don't you see, without being interrupted or bothered the way you are at home. We'll find rooms or an apartment or something. The boys said Spain is cheap."

"But—I cannot take your money, Francesca. You are good to offer, but I could not. I contribute nothing to the project."

"Oh, of course you do," said Francie. "I need you. You can manage to talk Spanish, can't you? Most Portuguese can, Maria said, or at least they can get along in the language, can't they?"

"Oh, yes, I can manage," said Catarina thoughtfully. She had forgotten that she was due back at the studio in about five minutes; her eyes were fixed on space. Encouraged, Francie went on talking. She drew alluring pictures of life in a foreign country. She pictured the two of them starting out on a new life, Catarina in search of fame and Francie after riches. Of course there were Catarina's children, but that could be arranged later. It all sounded so simple and attractive that Francie convinced herself as well as her audience. She could hardly wait to get started. Lisbon had treated both of them badly, she told herself. Very well, Lisbon would have to get along without them.

"But do you think we can simply drop out like that, so easily?" asked Catarina. "What about your father? What is he going to say when he hears? And Mrs. Barclay, won't she be insane with worry?"

"Of course I'll write to Aunt Lolly, as soon as we get there," said Francie, "and to Pop as well. As for the rest, I'd rather they didn't know. I'd rather they never, never find out." She was feeling miserable again. It was all very well to talk blithely about getting away, and never returning to Portugal, and all that, but it was going to be rather hard not to see Ruy and Maria ever again, and one or two of the others. Still, she reminded herself, she was ruined in Ruy's eyes already. There could be no doubt that Fontoura either had spoken to Ruy as he had done to Aunt Lolly, or that he would do it soon. Francie had lost face; she did not want to see the da Souzas. She was ashamed, as she was ashamed to face Aunt Lolly, knowing what she now knew. Besides, though she was quite sincere in her belief that she was doing the right thing about Catarina, you couldn't expect Catarina's relatives, such as Maria and Ruy, to approve of a girl who snatched a married woman right out of her home, and helped her to get away from her husband— even if he was cruel.

"Will you come, then, Catarina?" she said aloud.

Catarina clasped her hands. "Oh, I'd love to. I want to. I—yes, Francesca, I will do it. But how? Let's see what one needs. Passport—you have a passport?"

"Of course I have," said Francie, "and what's more, it's got a visa for Spain. Aunt Lolly thought we might want to go. What about yours?"

"I have the necessary papers. But Francesca— how? When?"

"You leave that to me," said Francie, with a bravado that was only half false. "There's a train that goes in the evening—I found out about it already at the American Express. This afternoon I'll get the tickets. And, Catarina, I don't like telephoning to your house. You give me a ring, will you, tonight after dinner? If you get Aunt Lolly first, don't tell her I didn't go back to class this afternoon."

Catarina still looked as if she didn't quite believe that all this was happening. She reached out and grasped

Francie's sleeve when the American started to get up.

"Francesca, you really mean it, don't you? I thought at first it was all a big joke. You do mean it?"

"You just turn up at the station at train time," said Francie, "and you'll see if I mean it or not."

CHAPTER 15

W ELL, that's over anyway," said Francie in carefully cheerful tones. Their taxi, an old one, bounced over the Barcelona cobblestones. She added after a brief pause, "Thank goodness," and stole a rather anxious glance at her companion.

Catarina did not reply. Her face as she looked out of the grimy window was expressionless, and Francie forced herself to go on chattering, though she didn't feel light-hearted. She was sleepy and worried. Still, she tried.

"It's wonderful to be here after hearing about it all these years. Don't you think so?" she demanded.

Catarina said, "Barcelona is not famous for its beauty."

"No, perhaps not, but the name itself sounds romantic," said Francie. "And it's a romantic city for us, Catarina. We're on an adventure. Doesn't that make a difference?"

Catarina rallied, and managed to smile. "Yes, that is true," she admitted.

The train journey had been dusty, hot and otherwise uncomfortable. What Francie had not bargained on was the power of little things to irritate. She had been quite ready to cope with important matters such as going through the customs, and changing money, and all that. What she had not expected was that the whole world should be surprised, amused and unpleasantly interested at the sight of two young women traveling about on their own. Everyone in the train seemed to think it queer. The men stared, or tried to make excuses to talk to them, and the women—but where were the women? Women didn't seem to do much traveling, Francie reflected.

Besides which, Catarina wasn't a good traveler. She was fussy and helpless at the same time. She needed a lot of waiting on, and she was touchy. No matter what innocent remark Francie might make on the train, Catarina seemed ready to take offense. When Francie complained about how annoying the little boys on the railway platform were, for instance, trying repeatedly to sell junky jewelry and plastic toys through the window, Catarina said,

"They are only trying to make a living. People in these countries are *poor*."

It made Francie feel that she had been haughty and spoiled in her behavior. And they even disagreed about two rakish young men with lacquered hair, who kept trying to scrape acquaintance with them.

"They make life so difficult," Francie had said in despair, after freezing them out for the third time. "They just don't seem to take no for an answer. I do think Portuguese men are extraordinary."

This offended Catarina. "They are very likely not Portuguese at all," she said, her eyes flashing with indignation. "I think they must be Spanish. And besides, you must remember, Francesca, that it is simply not done, what we are doing—traveling in this madcap fashion of yours, without chaperones or husbands. Those young men must be excused if they do not understand."

"I don't care what their nationality may be," said Francie irritably, "and I don't care if they understand or not. I just want them to leave me alone when I don't want an *apéritif*. I *don't* want an *apéritif*, and I don't want to talk to them either."

Catarina said she didn't, any more than Francie, and peace was restored.

But it was a long journey, they weren't able to sleep well because of arriving at the customs barrier at night, and altogether it was a great relief to have it over with, because Francie's conscience made a bad traveling companion. All too often in the night it had asked her just what she thought she was going to do about Catarina now she was there. It had seemed a fine idea at the time, a splendid, heroic gesture to get her away from her unhappy life. It was still a good idea, but other ideas clamored to be formed. What was Catarina to do with herself ultimately? Just paint?

"I'll take care of her," Francie reflected, "and in the end I suppose I can get her to America. Then Pop will be able to advise me."

But would Pop appreciate having a lovely young Portuguese matron left on his doorstep? And, if it came to that, how long would Catarina herself appreciate being cut off from her children? For all Francie knew, she was already beginning to brood about them, and to regret her action. Right now, bouncing in the Barcelona cab, she was probably regretting the whole thing bitterly. Nervously Francie watched the sensitive, worried face.

Catarina sighed sharply. "I have been thinking," she said. "I must send a telegram to my dressmaker. We had an appointment tomorrow. . . ."

Well, that was not so bad, thought Francie, and returned to her own problems. She had left a note for Mrs. Barclay, not on the traditional pincushion because, for one thing, there had been no pincushion in the hotel. But she left it in the mailbox downstairs, where it could not be missed.

"Darling Aunt Lolly: I heard you talking with Fontoura the other day at the party. I heard everything. I simply can't bear it any more in class, and so I'm going away for a while to think it all over. Please don't worry about me. You know I'm quite sensible and can take care of myself. Please don't bother Pop and tell him, either, until you hear from me. I'll be writing to you soon. Honestly I'm all right. With love, Francie."

Francie thought of this letter and was reassured. Aunt Lolly couldn't possibly worry about her. "Did you leave a note for your husband, Catarina?" she asked suddenly.

"Oh yes, naturally," said Catarina. "I left it on the pincushion."

This city of Barcelona was bewildering after so many hours of traveling through lonely landscape. The car took them to a street of hotels and restaurants that seemed in the muted light of evening to be swarming with all the people in the world. Francie marveled at the crowd.

"It's simply incredible," she said. "Hundreds of people, thousands of people. Where do they all come from?"

Catarina said, "The countryside was so empty. I suppose they all come here to work."

"They don't look as if they were working," said

Francie doubtfully. The car crawled slowly between strolling merrymakers—couples and groups of women in light summer dresses and men in white jackets. They looked a swarthy, tough people, she said. "And I'd know I wasn't in Portugal," she added. "They look different."

"Of course they are different," said Catarina with an indulgent smile. The Portuguese always insisted defiantly on this difference, Francie knew.

They had picked one certain hotel from the list offered them by the agency, because Catarina remembered that some of her relatives always stayed there when they visited Spain. It was one of Francie's few experiences with a hotel that wasn't purely a vacation concern such as Mrs. Barclay's in Estoril. This hotel was purely urban, and queerer than anything Francie could have imagined. Its doorway jostled for space with a café on one side and a cinema on the other, in the middle of a narrow, clamorous street. Their driver had some difficulty in getting a porter to come out and help with the bags, and when they themselves went through the doorway, Francie understood why. On the ground floor, all she could see of the hotel was an enormously high, narrow room of white stone, with a staircase and an elevator behind it. She paused and stared around her. No one was in sight.

"Where is it?" she asked Catarina.

The porter, a suitcase under each arm, motioned to them with his head to follow. Silently the young women walked after him to a little box of an elevator, lined with faded red plush. He pushed a button and they rose, very slowly, with ominous groans and shakes en route, past several floors.

"We're going right straight up to the roof," said Francie apprehensively.

Catarina remained calm. "The hotel is near the top of the building," she explained. "I have been in others like this. You will see."

The elevator box groaned and shook itself to a stop, behind an iron grille. They stepped out to dusty carpets leading to a reception desk in an awesome room. The ceiling was as high as that of the marble entry downstairs; a tall door showed a lounge full of deep, dark chairs and sofas; behind the desk, among a riot of letter boxes and niches, were twisted gilt lamps and statues. A disdainful young clerk looked inquiring. If Catarina had not stepped forward and assumed control, Francie would have fled. As it was, she stood her ground and even surrendered her passport when the clerk demanded it. "For the police," as Catarina explained. "They always keep the passport overnight."

If the Barcelona streets far below them had seemed stiflingly hot, their bedroom was far worse. Not the slightest breeze stirred the heavy lace curtain that masked a French window, as Francie went to investigate it. Outside a shallow balcony of grillwork stuck to the window like a fancy matchbox that was merely pasted on. She stepped out and looked down on the jammed, jostling street. Puffs of noise drifted up through the shadows. Night was falling, without coolness.

Francie sighed wearily. Now that the worst of the trip was over, she felt let down. She had done it; she was free, and so was Catarina. Life was beginning, but just at that moment it didn't seem as gay and light-hearted an affair as it had on the day before. If this was freedom, where had all the excitement of it gone? Warm as the night was, she shivered.

"A bath," she decided. "A bath will make all the difference."

Catarina lay on her narrow bed, utterly worn out. She moved only her eyes as Francie came in. "I am too tired to unpack," she said.

"Food's what we want," said Francie. "We'll have baths and then go out to some little restaurant. It's too late, I suppose, to call the boys tonight."

"No," said Catarina. "No restaurant, Francesca. Not just the two of us."

Francie was exasperated. She began, "But Catarina, I keep telling you. American girls go around alone, even in Spain. They—"

"I am not an American girl, and I cannot pretend

to be one," said Catarina firmly. "It is bad enough that we travel by ourselves—oh, I know it is not really bad, but it doesn't look well. If, on top of that, we go out at this hour, all alone, they might even ask us to leave the hotel. I am not sure, but it is possible. No, Francesca, we had better dine here."

"You mean in the hotel dining room?" asked Francie dolefully. Catarina nodded in a decided manner. "Oh dear," said Francie. "Well—all right. But I did want a good dinner in some special place."

"It would not be very good in any place," said Catarina, speaking like the lofty, proud Portuguese that she was. "These Spaniards cannot cook, so it doesn't matter."

They dined quietly in a square, whitewashed room, at a table covered with a dirty cloth. "I must not think about anything," Francie cautioned herself. "I'll just be upset if I do. Much better to wait until morning, when everything will look easier."

Disconsolate nevertheless, she went to bed soon after dinner. The noise and laughter of the streets seemed louder, once the lights were turned off. For a long time she lay wakeful on her hard pillow, hearing in the streets the happy chatter of people she didn't know.

It would be no use ringing anyone up, said Catarina in the morning, until ten o'clock at least; these Southern peoples went to bed late and they rose late to make up for it. Francie tried to adapt herself. She stayed in bed, as she had almost never done in Estoril. Like Catarina, she drank a cup of whipped chocolate that tasted too sweet, and she was very slow in dressing. Still, it was only half-past nine when she was ready to go out.

She was half afraid Catarina would still insist that two lone women could not appear in public. But it seemed that these annoying rules of conduct were relaxed in the daytime. Accordingly the girls sauntered around the bright, hot streets near the hotel, looking in shop windows stocked with dolls dressed as toreadors, or with little gilt bulls, or fans with bull-fighting motifs painted on them.

"Pretty crummy stuff," said Francie.

"For the tourists, I suppose," said Catarina.

It was getting very warm, and they walked slower than ever on their way back to the hotel. Now at last they could make a telephone call. It was a very exposed proceeding, at the reception desk. Francie had to give Jimmy's name and address at the top of her voice, and the clerk repeated the information in a loud shout to a girl at a switchboard, who was concealed in a little back room. She yelled the number back at him, and by means of such dialogue, translated with difficulty by Catarina, they learned at last that the two young American men had gone to the seaside for several days.

"At Costa Brava," Catarina explained. "It is the nearest nice *plage*, and most people go there for holidays. There is a telephone at their house there. Do you wish to try again to reach them?"

Francie wiped her face and nodded, and the painful process of telephoning was repeated. While the hidden maiden put the call through, the clerk leaned on the desk and pared his nails, staring at Francie and Catarina as if he had never seen women before. It was a cheerful, unabashed stare without any self-consciousness about it. Francie supposed that in time she would get used to that sort of thing, but for the moment it made her very nervous. Catarina, on the other hand, seemed unperturbed, as if the clerk did not exist. Francie resolved to imitate that gracefully careless manner if it took her years to learn it. To begin with, she did as Catarina had done—picked up a travel folder from the desk and flicked the pages, just as if she could read them. But she knew she wasn't as good at it as her model: Catarina really wasn't aware of the clerk, and Francie was—painfully.

Her musings were interrupted by the surprising news, after a long wait, that the call was through. In a tiny telephone box she listened for Jimmy's voice, and there, all of a sudden, it was. He sounded astonished.

"Whatever are you doing in Spain? Did your aunt

decide on the trip after we left, or what?" he demanded.

"It's a long story," said Francie. "I'm not with Aunt Lolly. How long before you come back to town?" Her mind was racing ahead. This was a serious complication, if her only friends were going to be out of touch. What could she do? Travel on to Paris? But her money was limited.

To her relief, Jimmy was saying, "Oh, my dear, we'll be back tomorrow. It was one of those long week ends, that's all. Will needed a rest, or thought he did. You aren't rushing straight out of town or anything like that, I hope. I'm curious to know what you're doing, and that's understating the case."

"Well, I warn you fair and square. To begin with, I want work," said Francie.

"We'll talk about it tomorrow. Good-by, now." Had there been a slight sound of dismay in his tone?

"I think it's all fascinating. Perfectly fascinating," said Will, his eyes roaming disparagingly around the café. His tone was languid, as always.

Jimmy showed more enthusiasm. "You're quite a girl, Francie. Not everybody would have done it— simply scooped up an accomplice and come away." He sat back and looked at her, grinning. "And to think *we* brought the whole thing down on your poor little head," he said thoughtfully. "Tempting you into the wrong ways, out of the pure realm of art."

"Poppycock," said Will Adams violently.

Jimmy said, "I don't know. This fellow Fontoura is right, in a way. The girl *is* better fitted for our racket than his."

"I'm not fitted for any one racket," said Francie hotly. "I can design, and I can paint, too. I don't see why anyone has to be stuck in one pigeonhole or another. Catarina doesn't either, and let me tell you, Catarina knows a lot about painting. Even Fontoura admits that. She says—"

"By the way, where *is* this wench?" asked Jimmy.

"Oh, I left her upstairs until we'd had our talk," said Francie. "I'll get her down in a minute."

There was a pause. "Well, I don't know, Dear Mysterious," said Jimmy at last. "We can't give you a job outright, of course. We don't operate that way." Adams grunted assent. "But if you want to snoop round and try your hand at more designs, you'll probably strike it right now and then," he went on. "I don't know how much work you need, or how long you can manage on this arrangement. . . . You'd better find rooms instead of this place, first thing." He frowned worriedly. "Frankly, it's not a thing I'd like to consider my responsibility," he said.

"I think you're both heading for trouble. But it's not my affair. Now, where's Catarina?"

As Francie went upstairs to get Catarina, she entered the bedroom tempestuously. Catarina, sitting scribbling at the little gimcrack desk, started as the door opened, and Francie thought that she blushed. But she collected herself quickly.

"You have seen your friends?" she asked in calm tones. She folded the paper on which she had been writing, and tucked it into her handbag.

"Yes, I have, and they're still downstairs." If she doesn't want me to see what she's doing, thought Francie as she spoke, it's all right with me. "We thought perhaps you'd like a cup of coffee with us. Would you?"

"Why not?" said Catarina. She patted her hair and announced herself ready.

The café was filling up with people who seemed to have a good deal of time on their hands, though it was still early in the morning. The designers seemed suitably impressed by Catarina's dramatic beauty, and Francie felt gratified, as if she had produced a work of art. As her friends all talked together, she began at last to experience the thrill she had waited for in vain, ever since leaving Lisbon. This really was Life, she told herself. There they were, she and Catarina, in Barcelona of all places, embarked on the Unknown.

And it was all, all her own doing. She was really making her mark on the world; she was causing things to happen. A flood of self-confidence filled her.

"Well, for crying out loud!" The words, in a cheerful American voice that was oddly familiar, floated across the café. Francie forced herself to ignore them. Barcelona was full of tourists, and it was no use getting excited over every American voice she heard. But then she turned around swiftly. The voice was saying, "Francie! Francie Nelson! It *is* you, isn't it?"

Francie saw the speaker and cried out, "Bob Chapman! What are you doing here?"

"I'll ask you that first," said Bob. He came striding among the little tables and grabbed both her hands. "Gee, it's good to see you," he said.

"This is Bob Chapman from my home town," Francie announced to her party as she made the introductions. "I haven't seen him since schooldays."

"When I darned near got this girl kicked out of school in England," said Bob cheerfully. "Remember that? Heard from Penny lately?"

"No, Penny's a bad letter-writer," said Francie. "Do sit down with us, Bob, and let's compare notes."

But for the first few minutes, Bob did most of the talking. First he had to tell the others all about Francie at Fairfields, and how he and Glenn had taken her out for a forbidden ride in their car. Then he explained that he was in Barcelona on an organized tour of Spain. "People laugh at these tours, but they're the best way to see the country when you're on your own," he said, "and I don't stick to the crowd unless I specially want to. But Francie, tell me about you. What are you doing here? I heard you were in Portugal."

"I was," said Francie after a short pause, "and then I came on here. To—to see the country."

Bob looked at her thoughtfully, but if he noticed her confusion he didn't show it. Instead he turned and glanced at Catarina, and then at the two other Americans. Francie had never realized before what shrewd eyes he had. "Where are your friends—that nice woman, Mrs. Barclay, or what's-her-name?" he asked.

"Everyone asks me that," thought Francie irritably. "Aunt Lolly's still in Portugal," she said. "The climate's better for her arthritis."

"I see. . . . Any chance of contacting you again before we move on? Our buses are staying here a couple of days," said Bob.

"We'll be in this hotel tonight, anyway," said Francie slowly. "But Catarina and I hope to find something else. Something cozier."

"Oh, it won't be hard," Jimmy assured her. "I know one or two places you might consider. If you're really staying, that is."

Francie wished he had not said that. She could feel Bob's eyes examining her again; she could imagine that he was wondering what was up. But never mind all that; it was marvelous, she decided, to meet somebody from home. She asked him eagerly about the gang. She didn't quite want to talk about Glenn, but Bob would notice if she didn't, and he might think she was sensitive about the engagement, so she said,

"How's Glenn?"

"Oh, he's fine. I saw him the day I left, as a matter of fact," said Bob. "The whole crowd came to see me off."

The whole crowd? It was on the tip of Francie's tongue to ask him to give her a list of the crowd, but that would have looked really pointed, and she resisted the impulse.

Bob looked at his watch and jumped up. "I've got to be back in time for lunch or there won't be any," he said. "Well, good-by for now." He looked around once more at the table, and added, "I'll try to find you later on, Francie." Then he walked out quickly, so that people looked after him. Almost nobody walked quickly at that time of day, in Barcelona. You could tell he was American, reflected Francie, if you were two blocks away.

The Americans of her own party were talking with Catarina about rooms. They would come back and take the girls out to find something, they said, after the post-lunch siesta.

"It's awfully nice of you," said Francie. "I didn't want to bother you so much."

"It's no bother," Jimmy assured her. But she thought he still looked worried.

CHAPTER 16

Do YOU mind a personal question, Miss Mysterious?"

Francie turned to look inquiringly at Jimmy, because his tone was grave. They had reached the door of the house where she and Catarina were now living, and she had intended to say good-by without inviting him in for coffee. She was tired after a day of walking through museums.

"Why—no, Jimmy, of course I don't mind. That is, unless you are going to be disagreeable." She laughed in a somewhat forced way.

"Oh no. I was just wondering if you'd written yet to Mrs. Barclay, to tell her where you are."

Francie was relieved, and her voice showed it. "Oh, that! Yes, I did write. In fact, I wrote nearly a week ago, as soon as we moved out of the hotel and I had a regular address."

They paused in the shadow of the doorway. The old woman who looked after the house shuffled to her door to peer out at them. "It's all right," called Jimmy. She knew him, so she disappeared.

"That's all right, then," said Jimmy. "The thing is, I got to wondering about talk getting back to her. We're not so far from Lisbon. You keep running into people in our crowd, and I figured there were bound to be some of them who know your Uncle Martin, if not his wife. Didn't that Mrs. Angus say something to you yesterday about your aunt?"

"Yes, she knows her. Met her in Paris. Poor Jimmy, with two problem girls on his hands," said Francie. He had started her off on a train of thought that was becoming familiar. "It's funny, you know, that Aunt Lolly hasn't answered my letter," she said. "I wonder why. It's not like her to get peeved or sulky."

"The mails may be slow," said Jimmy. "Well, I'll be running along. I've got to get back. Look here, don't take it too hard that Will didn't care for that last thing you sent him. You can't always hit the ball in this game."

"Oh, I know that. I don't mind in the least," said Francie, and smiled at him brilliantly and falsely. The rejection *had* upset her a good deal, though she knew in theory that it would be impossible to sell every single thing she offered. Never mind, she told herself again, life just isn't that smooth.

By the time she had gone up the stairs to her door, she was feeling more cheerful. It never took Francie long to reassure herself, so she was unprepared for what she found in the darkly shuttered living room—Catarina prone on the lumpy little green sofa, sobbing her heart out.

Francie ran over to her. "Catarina! Whatever is the matter?"

Catarina shook her head violently and cried harder than ever. At last, however, she pushed herself up to a sitting position and wiped her eyes.

"He never writes," she said.

Francie was really mystified. "Who doesn't write?" she asked. "I didn't know you wanted—"

"My husband."

"But how could he? He doesn't know where you are," said Francie. As a matter of fact, however, she had been puzzled once or twice, when she stopped to think, about Catarina's husband. Surely if he had wanted to he would have been able to find out, long since, where they were. The police kept records in both countries of all travelers' passports.

But that was not what Catarina meant. "He knows, he knows," she said, as fresh tears welled up to her eyes and rolled out. "I wrote and told him."

"You *did*?"

"Of course I did, as soon as we got here. Do you think that so strange, Francesca? Yes, I can see that you do. You Americans never understand the *heart*. You are cold. Oh, he is cruel not to write. It is his mother—" Sobs interrupted her.

Just then, while poor Francie's brain was still in a muddle over this reversal of her ideas of Catarina and what Catarina wanted, there came a knock at the door. It was a bold, different sort of knock; it could not have been the old woman.

"Come in!" she said, forgetting that she was in Spain. The door opened, and Francie blinked. There stood a man she had never seen before, a very young, shy-looking man with sensitive features. Beyond him, looming up by his shoulder was—of all people—Ruy da Souza.

Francie had only a minute to goggle. With a shrill scream, Catarina leaped across the room and threw herself at the strange young man. As she approached it seemed to Francie that he looked embarrassed.

"What I still don't understand," Francie was saying, an hour later, "is Catarina. That poor boy isn't a bit like what she described. I thought her husband was a perfect monster, from all she said."

"I know," said Ruy. "That—well, that is Catarina. She has a strong imagination." Francie waited, but he had said all he meant to say on that subject.

"I hope I haven't made too much trouble," she added tentatively, to stir him up.

Ruy said briefly that she had not exactly helped matters in the de Abreu family. "However," he added, relenting when he saw her distress, "it is never a smooth life for any of Catarina's family. At least you have not made matters much worse. We all know Catarina, you see. She can't help it, but she likes drama. She is a very talented girl, but she does like drama. Things happen to Catarina. If it hadn't been you, it would have been someone else." Ruy sighed, and then said more briskly, "But as for yourself, I think you have been very unkind to Mrs. Barclay. You must not be offended if I speak frankly. She was worried to death."

Francie said, "Ruy, are you sure? Or are you just saying that because you think she ought to have been worried?"

"She was most anxious," said Ruy firmly. "We all were. Naturally, as soon as my cousin learned of his wife's escapade, we knew you were all right, in a way. We knew where you were. But to live alone in a large Spanish city! If my cousin's mother scolds Catarina, this one time she will be justified. It was a reckless thing to do."

Subdued, Francie did not fire up and defend Catarina's rights, or her own. She had seldom been at such a disadvantage. They sat quietly for a minute or two. Like most of Barcelona at that moment they were in the Ramblas, a place in the middle of the city where everyone comes to walk or sip sweet drinks or shop. Ruy had selected a little café where there was room for only two tables in front of the door, and they sat at one of them, crowded against the wall with very little space for their legs and feet. People passed and repassed a bare six inches, it seemed, in front of their noses.

Back in the girls' rooms, Francie knew, Catarina was alternately weeping and packing, while her husband stood around trying to help. For the first time in that crowded hour, Francie began to wonder how things had happened to turn out in just this way. She could understand that Catarina's husband would have come straight to Catarina's address as soon as he was able, but why was Ruy here? Francie asked him.

"Oh, he wanted someone from the family to be with him, of course," said Ruy.

Of course? Francie pondered, as she had often done before, on the amazing clan spirit of her friends in Portugal. They always seemed to do everything in numbers, even to tracing down a missing wife. You would have thought that this one matter, she reflected, could be handled alone by a husband. But even Catarina didn't seem to resent having Ruy as an audience; she was probably used to it.

"I was chosen to accompany him," continued Ruy. "It was my father's suggestion." Ruy paused here so long that Francie turned to look at him. His

face was bent toward hers and he gazed at her mean-
ingly. "*My father* himself suggested it," he repeated.
"Do you know what that means?"

No, Francie didn't.

"Ah, well," said Ruy. He sat back, and said as if
at a tangent, "I went to see Mrs. Barclay before we
started out."

"That was kind of you, Ruy."

"But of course I did. She was most relieved that
something was being done. You—really, Francesca,
forgive me for repeating this, but you do not seem to
appreciate her. She is fond of you. Very fond."

Francie saw no necessity to go on protesting. Ruy
just didn't know. But she took heart: Aunt Lolly
would understand, thank goodness. She always did.

Ruy cleared his throat and continued. "I spoke
to Mrs. Barclay quite frankly. It seemed only right
that I should do so, before speaking to you. I am sure
you agree."

He seemed to be waiting for something. Francie, absorbed in her thoughts, did not reply. Ruy said a little
louder, "You do agree, do you not? It was correct
for me to ask her first. She stands in the place of your
mother, Francesca. And I have never met your father,
though of course I have written him as well."

Francie heard him now, but she was bewildered.
"What about?" she asked. "What did you ask Aunt
Lolly?"

"Why," said Ruy, "about our marriage, of course. Yours and mine."

Really, Francie said to herself at first, this is just too much. Two big shocks in one afternoon . . .

It seemed hours before she could speak. In that time she managed to readjust her thoughts a little. Ruy was proposing! Actually proposing marriage. It was, practically, Francie's first proposal—you could hardly count the way boys at home sometimes talked. So this was what it was like. Well, she could hardly say that she had expected it, not just in this way, and not so abruptly. Ruy was a very strange boy. She hoped he didn't care too much, because she knew already, without having to think it over, that she wouldn't accept.

She found words, though they were hardly adequate. "What did Aunt Lolly say?" she asked in a small voice.

"Not very much. Of course she is American, and I could not have expected her to be different. She said it was your affair." Ruy sounded faintly surprised by this, and Francie surprised him further.

"Ruy, I'm so sorry. It's awfully sweet of you, but—" She stopped, overcome by how silly she sounded. This was a proposal, a serious matter. You don't tell a man he is being sweet when he proposes. "It's *darling* of you," she went on, though that didn't sound much better, "it's perfectly darling of you, but I can't. I don't want to get married at all."

Ruy looked amazed. "Don't want to?" he repeated. It seemed a brand-new idea.

"After all," said Francie, "I'm rather young to be getting married."

"Yes, all that, but . . . my dear Francesca, don't you realize? You *must* get married," said Ruy. "After running away, and everybody knowing. There is no possible way we could hush it up. You simply must. Can't you see?"

"I can't see at all," said Francie. "You mean people in Lisbon are talking about me?"

Words seemed to fail Ruy. She had to guess from his expression how much people were talking.

"But it doesn't matter!" cried Francie. "I mean, not enough to get married on! Oh dear, Ruy, was that the reason you proposed? The only reason?"

All her first flattered thoughts were thrown into confusion. Ruy was just being a gentleman. He thought he had to protect her.

"There is no need to put it like that, Francesca. I told you, my father himself—*my father*—was agreeable to my coming to fetch you." Ruy spoke almost with awe. "You see what that means. He will call on Mrs. Barclay to talk matters over, as soon as you are safely back in Estoril. And then, of course, your father will want to meet him. I suppose that can be arranged next time my father goes to America. I will accompany him, and I think we should decide to make this trip very soon. You must not be forced to live in a hostile environment, all alone, for too long. I think—"

"Ruy, please wait a minute," begged Francie. "You're going too fast. Ruy, do listen. Believe me, I can't marry you. None of this is necessary. I do appreciate it, I am grateful, and I'm sure Aunt Lolly is, too. But my Pop would never want me to marry you in all this hurry, just because some old cats in Lisbon are talking about me."

It took a long time to convince him. He seemed rather insulted at the end. But Francie prevailed, and though she consented to return to Portugal with the party, she was firm about the engagement.

They bought tickets for the very next day; there was just time to telephone Will and Jimmy, to explain.

"Oh, that's *splendid*," said Jimmy when he heard. "I mean, of course, I'm sorry we won't be seeing you again, but we meant to pull out pretty soon ourselves, to Venice, and I must say I had you on my mind. Well, all's well that ends well, isn't it? And remember, we must meet again in New York. You'll carry on with your work, won't you? Let me hear from you, then."

"I'm so sorry, Aunt Lolly. I'm *so* sorry."
Mrs. Barclay looked thoughtful. "I'm sure you

are, my dear. It wasn't a very intelligent thing to do, now was it?"

"It was silly," Francie admitted, "but honestly, I did feel so terrible. Still, running away didn't help anything, and it was awfully childish—and selfish, too. I got everyone terribly upset! Oh Aunt Lolly, maybe someday I'll learn to take things like a grownup should!"

"There was no need to get hysterical, that's true," said Aunt Lolly severely. "But there, I can hardly blame you, remembering some of the things that little painter said."

"Yes . . ." Francie hesitated, wondering where all her former anger and grief had gone. It seemed such a long time ago, and so much had happened since, that she could hardly understand, herself, what it had been like. "Anyway, I guess I've thought it out," she said, "and I'm not so disappointed any more. I do know now that I'm good for something, anyway. I learned quite a lot more about textiles and patterns in Spain; Jimmy was terribly good about showing me round. When I get back to America I'm going to concentrate on learning about designing."

"That's nice," said Aunt Lolly absently. She was sitting at her desk, shuffling through papers. "Francie, did you write to your father right away, or send him a telegram, or what?"

"Pop? Oh, I didn't tell him. I didn't want to bother him," said Francie.

Mrs. Barclay said, "But he knows!"

"Aunt Lolly, how could he know? I didn't tell him."

"He cabled me," said Mrs. Barclay. "He's been cabling regularly for several days. I was sure you had written. Now, how in the world? Oh, here's some mail for you, too, and a telegram from your father."

OUGHT TO GIVE YOU GOOD SHAKING BUT WON'T, Pop had cabled. CONGRATULATIONS NEW CAREER COME HOME SOON BY THE WAY WHO IS RUY DA SOUZA LOVE

Francie folded the flimsy paper and looked up at Aunt Lolly with happy eyes. "That makes me feel so much better, I'd like to jump up and yell," she said.

"I think his affairs are running smooth again," said Mrs. Barclay. "He wrote to me about all this. He's really awfully proud of you, Francie, for having made this effort for yourself—the patterns, I mean, not the running away. Though even that—" She checked herself. "He's not as angry as he might be," she admitted.

Francie had opened a letter and was reading it, listening to Aunt Lolly with only half her attention.

"Mark is coming over to tea," Aunt Lolly said.

"Oh, yes, Mark. I only hope *he* won't start trying

to save my reputation by sacrificing himself," said Francie. "No, never mind, Aunt Lolly, I'll tell you about all that later. Oh, now I know how Pop found out. I saw Bob Chapman in Barcelona, and he thought something was funny about me being there, and he seems to have cabled Glenn. What a nerve!"

"So Glenn told your father," said Mrs. Barclay.

"Yes, right away. I can't find anything in this letter about his engagement," said Francie. "This is Glenn's letter. . . . Oh, here it is. My goodness! Listen to this, Aunt Lolly. 'Your friend Gretta is engaged to a man from out of town. Seems she's been keeping him under her hat for several months.' So that was it! I thought it was sort of funny that Glenn wouldn't tell me if he was engaged." She looked out of the window at the sea. "I'm glad," she said. "He's too young to be engaged. So am I, for that matter. So is Mark—and Ruy. There's plenty of time."

Aunt Lolly said, "But not much time left for Portugal. We're starting home in a week, you know. What were you saying about Ruy?"

"I'll tell you later," said Francie. "He *is* nice. But there's plenty of time."

She went on looking dreamily at the sea.